Dedicated to my children Melanie, Renee, and Alin.

If you enjoyed this book please review this book on the website from which you purchased it or at goodreads.com. We thank all who take the time to review and rate this book in advance THANK YOU.

ELYSIAN FIELDS

By Anne Gabriels

Published by ELSE Inc.
Copyright © 2014 by ELSE Inc. on behalf of the author.

ELSE Inc.
Suite 354
13,300 Tecumseh Rd E
Tecumseh, Ontario, Canada
    N8N 4R8

publishing.info@elseinc.com

Kindle ISBN: 978-0-9920414-3-4
Ebook ISBN: 978-0-9920414-4-1
Hardcover ISBN: 978-0-9920414-2-7
Paperback ISBN: 978-0-9920414-5-8

Banning human cloning reflects our humanity. It is the right thing to do. Creating a child through this new method calls into question our most fundamental beliefs. It has the potential to threaten the sacred family bonds at the very core of our ideals and our society. At its worst, it could lead to misguided and malevolent attempts to select certain traits, even to create certain kind of children -- to make our children objects rather than cherished individuals.

BILL CLINTON, speech, June 9, 1997

Anybody who objects to cloning on principle has to answer to all the identical twins in the world who might be insulted by the thought that there is something offensive about their very existence. Clones are simply identical twins.

RICHARD DAWKINS, BBC interview, Jan. 31, 1999

Editor's Note

When I was in college, I was reading the university paper while eating lunch one day, when I saw an article on human cloning. Too many years have gone by and I no longer remember what it was about, but I do remember the article struck a serious nerve with me. My mind buzzed as I walked to my chemistry class, where I would spend the next hour furiously scribbling out a response instead of taking notes. Human cloning was wrong and I outlined several reasons why, including a new breed of "racism," the degradation of the value of human life, the impossibility of cloning the soul, and the difficulties even the possibility of cloning would have on criminal prosecution relying on DNA evidence.

Later that day, after fine tuning my draft, I emailed my response to the newspaper. I felt better having said my piece and went on with school.

I found out later that they published my letter, and it was a moment of pride for me. I'd felt so strongly that cloning humans was wrong that I needed my voice to be heard. It seems an odd twist of fate that over a decade later, I'd meet Anne and become her editor for Elysian Fields, a book that explores many of the same ethical dilemmas I'd taken issue with.

Being a big fan of dystopian literature, there are a lot of fictional worlds out there that can scare and inspire us, but the ones that tie back to our own beliefs are the ones that affect us the most. Anne's book presents one such situation to me personally. While people such as myself may believe that human cloning is inherently wrong, it doesn't mean it won't happen.

Nor does it mean we won't have to deal with all the effects I outlined in my letter all those years ago. Let's just hope societies such as that of Elysian Fields remain happily in the realm of fiction for just a bit longer.

Crystal Watanabe

Prelude

Elysian Fields deserved its name. It was an island of beauty, at least for the dominant Elite class; a place considered a blessing from God because it kept them alive, even after the great cataclysm of half a century ago. The city was built after the Great Quakes on the western outskirts of a once great city, bordered by a lake to the north, its skyscrapers still visible. It rested behind a tall forest they had planted using accelerated growth hormones, eager to be rid of the ugliness of the ruined buildings.

The one hundred and twenty thousand Elysians, though a mere fraction of the former population, would have expanded the city further, but they were blocked by the fog. The entire city was surrounded by it. The forest obscured the heavy mist, but it was there, a mile or so into the lake, and it looked like a large, milky wall reaching up to the sky around both the old and the new city. Impenetrable and always present, it had terrified them. Venturing too far into the fog resulted in psychological panic and thus all who tried were forced to return. After decades, they got used to it and their children did not even know a life without the ring of fog.

The people of Elysian Fields liked to keep order in the city, so that everyone knew their place in the society. Four distinct classes provided that order.

The Elites formed the upper class. Less than a thousand, they owned businesses and lived in large mansions based on English architecture within exclusive guarded communities, enjoying fresh foods supplied by their own gardens and livestock. They showed great interest in prolonging their life and health through technological enhancements. They benefited from advancements in nano-technology and genetic engineering. Embryonic cell manipulation provided them with their own clones, kept in stasis and ready to be harvested or, in extreme cases, to replace the originals too deteriorated to survive transplants.

Around twenty thousand Professionals comprised the middle class. They maintained and operated the autonomous factories and performed research in various high-tech fields including biomedical sciences, nano-technology, genetic engineering, gaming, and virtual reality entertainment. Professionals also maintained the intra-city network, which they called the hypernet. They lived in fashionable neighborhoods and were able to afford some of the benefits the Elites were enjoying such as medical care, good education, particularly in the technical and medical fields, and occasionally fresh produce.

The Servers constituted the lower class, a large mass of people with the role to serve both the Elites and the Professionals. They lived either in their own compound, in rows of low apartment buildings, or with the Elites or Professionals employing them. Their children took online classes due to their various places of residence. Their favorite pastime was entering the world of entertainment, a welcome escape from the confines of their small world and their otherwise dull existence. Food, processed in the autonomous factories, was inexpensive and they could have almost as much as they wanted while watching their shows and games.

And then there were the Scrappies, very hard to quantify, though not numbering more than a few hundred. They lived on the fringe of society and were not officially acknowledged as a class, rather tolerated. Occasionally, a Scrappie would be caught stealing something or becoming annoying one way or another and would be taken to the Happy Endings clinic to be terminated in a humane way. Anyone who ran away from one of the classes, for various reasons, became a Scrappie. It was unheard of for a Scrappie to rise to another class, but occasionally some of them would go back home. Clones lived with them as well; some were unwanted experiments left alive due to a nurse's pity, while others were discarded doubles of deceased people whose relatives did not want them around anymore but could not bring themselves to have them disposed of. They were allowed to live on the other side of the forest, close to the center of the former city of skyscrapers, but occasionally they would venture into the city, scavenging for food.

After fifty years of isolation, the Elysians could not even imagine a life outside their beloved city.

PART ONE

1

Allan entered the square and hurried towards the Imaginarium building, a geodesic dome placed in the middle of the Elite Plaza, where he was going to meet with his friends, Brad and Brent.

The building hosted three dimensional movie theatres and video arcades equipped with the latest equipment. A lot of Elite youngsters spent considerable amounts of time in the totally immersive experiences the complex had to offer. The main attraction was the new virtual reality game *War of Sovereign Nations*.

At nineteen, Allan was six-foot two inches tall, fit and healthy, and he was in perfect shape due to regular nanobot treatments. He lived with his Father, the head of Secure-IT, originally an information technology company and for as long as Allan could remember, the only security company in the city, employing over five hundred security personnel responsible for keeping order in the city.

"Hey," Allan announced his presence. "You guys ready for the challenge?"

"You're late. I thought you'd already thrown in the towel and admitted defeat," teased Brad, offering a gleaming white smile in contrast to his light brown complexion.

"Let's go, already," Brent, a sandy brown haired youth, said impatiently. "Our booked time has already started." They headed in the direction of the arcades.

They entered a spacious oval-shaped room with various consoles placed in an arc on both sides of the door. The opposite wall was massive and comprised the exterior wall of the Imaginarium building. It served as a screen designed for three dimensional viewing. At least, Allan thought so, because the image he saw was distorted, a clear sign that special viewers were needed to bring the picture into focus.

"What do you want to do, play against each other or against the computer?" Brent asked them.

"Playing against each other is faster and more fun," Brad suggested.

"Yeah, but we don't know anything about this game. Let's test it for a while, see what it can do. We can all play against the computer, like they advertised on the hypernet, each of us on a different front, and see who wins more points." Allan's suggestion sounded good, and the others accepted immediately.

They moved towards different consoles and stood in front of them. Special gloves were placed in supports mounted on both sides of each unit to enable them to manipulate the holographic controls, and hyper-goggles were hanging from a hook nearby to facilitate a complete view of the war zones and the map.

Allan put on the goggles and the gloves and selected the option of playing against the computer on section C, which had been assigned to his console. He saw his friends doing the same on their respective locations.

All of a sudden, the large screen in front of them came to life in a multitude of flashing colors, displaying the overall map of the playing field, and Allan could hear a man's voice:

"Welcome to the *War of Sovereign Nations* game. You selected Option 1 – War against the *Emperor* by individual *Warlords*. You can go to the *Menu* at any time to change your options. Each nation is assigned a separate front of action. The winner is the warlord who conquers the most, with the least damage and the greatest profit.

Allan determined that the *Emperor* must be the computer. *Cool, I'm a Warlord. Let's see what we have here.* He started to look at all the various options he had in order to initiate war; he had an arsenal, troops, the cities, and the terrain he had to conquer. He tried to gather as much insight into his enemy's resources and strongholds as he was allowed via his console's controls.

In the meantime, Brad and Brent had already started. *Wow, these guys are in a hurry to beat me.* This did not deter Allan from analyzing the situation in order to come up with a strategy, like his father had taught him. *Victorious warriors win first and then go to war, while defeated warriors go to war first and then seek to win.* That was one of the lessons from the *Art of War*, one of his father's prized classics, developed by the ancient Chinese general Sun-Tzu. *We'll see who the best is in the end.* And Allan continued his analysis.

After he finished his assessment, Allan was still uncertain as to how to proceed. He knew his best bet was to engage people with what they expect; it is what they are able to discern and confirms their projections. It settles them into predictable patterns of response, occupying their minds while you wait for the extraordinary moment — that which they cannot anticipate. *What is the Emperor expecting?* He wasn't sure. Probably to be attacked in full force. He had no idea yet as to what surprise attack he could execute without alerting the Emperor. *What are Brad and Brent doing?* Allan glanced at the overall battlefield to try and understand the way his friends were waging war.

It was easy to anticipate Brad's strategy. He was a proponent of traditional warfare. He said no to nuclear attacks and just stuck with plain air attacks supported by sea carriers. He maintained control over supplies and sea routes, followed by ground troop attacks.

The reaction from the computer would be predictable: a huge loss of life on both sides, great destruction of human artifacts and an uncertain victory, since the people living there would not give up easily. The three dimensional images had already started to show the utter devastation of the cities, the fireworks of explosions in various locations, and Allan anticipated a total loss of control on both sides of their armies and battle fronts.

There is no instance of a country having benefited from prolonged warfare. How well Allan remembered that. His father had told him stories deeply embedded in his mind of episodes in the history of mankind, from before the Great Quakes. So many people had lost their lives in extended wars. One of them was said to have lasted a hundred years. *What a waste!*

A look at the other war showed Allan what his other friend was doing. Brent had attempted cyber-attacks, similar to what happened in the first part of the century: infecting the web with Trojans that would upload viruses to create havoc in communication, threaten self-destruction of the power plants, plot to bring down the financial system and cause breaches of government sites, mostly for the retrieval of sensitive military information.

The three dimensional representation of that war showed that the disruption was great. Anarchy had already begun to set in as a couple of nuclear plants exploded accidentally. The contamination would be unimaginable, with many areas uninhabitable for generations. *Brent's scenario will end in a stalemate,* Allan thought, with an odd feeling of grief. *Why would he do that? That's madness.* He shuddered thinking that such a thing could perhaps have happened to the planet, to bring it to the current state.

What am I going to do? What is the best way to conquer a country? Suddenly, Allan remembered the quote: *The skillful leader subdues the enemy's troops without any fighting; he captures their cities without laying siege to them; he overthrows their kingdom without lengthy operations in the field.*

In the practical art of war, the best thing was to take the enemy's country whole and intact; to shatter and destroy it was not ideal, for what use would it be after? What did he truly want? To take control of that country. Brute force was less effective than deceit. He could attempt to take the country from them while keeping them with their guard down, not expecting what was coming to them, making them feel safe and secure, fed and entertained. While he set things in motion, his own peons in positions of authority in the country would do the job for him.

Allan thought about it and decided that, strange as it seemed, he was going to invest his virtual money into buying and developing entertainment networks, infusing them with irresistible shows and interactive games, and supplying very affordable food to the target country. The people would spend their spare time greatly entertained and well fed. The entertainment would distract them and the food would be laced with addictive chemicals, dulling their senses and causing them to become lethargic and less aware of what was truly happening to their country.

It took some programming on Allan's part to change the behavioral subroutines and though it took longer for the simulation to run, he made quick work of it. The images on the large screen showed life as usual, except for the slow approach of his war carriers, pretending to conduct routine military exercises. At the time his troops landed, they were received with indifference by the local population, who couldn't care less, one way or the other, as long as their lifestyle went unchanged. *But it would change,* Allan thought with unexpected bitterness. There were no casualties on his side, even some profit from the economical trades.

The final score was displayed. Allan had won hands down.

"I can't believe it," Brad exclaimed, looking at Allan in frustration, while removing his gloves and hyper-googles. "What the heck did you do? I didn't see any real action taking place. Did you hack into the game?"

"He must have," Brent intervened. "I saw him writing code. Hey, Allan, is this what you're trained to do at Secure-IT? Win by changing the rules of the game?"

Allan could understand very well the disappointment of his friends, even their anger. They were not used to losing, especially without understanding how it had happened. Even he felt a slight disappointment at the result. Somehow, he thought the game would be more challenging.

"The only thing I did was trick the enemy into thinking no war was going on. I manipulated the people's minds, that's all. I didn't think it would be so damn easy. But, hey, I won."

"You won by cheating, that's what you did. There was no war in your game," Brad replied, with disappointment in his voice. "We should have established better rules, like playing using similar technologies, and see whose strategy would win the war. Now there's no fair way to compare our results."

"You're right. We should play against each other next time. We can set a time period, like early nineteen hundreds, so we can pick only the types of guns available then and let the best man win," Allan said, trying to appease his friends. They both nodded in agreement, rather quietly and slightly withdrawn, as if affected by the virtual destruction they caused, only to be defeated.

They left the oval room and the three dimensional image on the wall behind them, with its bright, blurred letters pulsing: *Game over. Play again (Y/N)?*

Together they left the Imaginarium and then separated, each of them going towards their respective homes.

Wearing the latest model of hyper-goggles, ear buds attached, Allan enjoyed the evening walk – one eye on a match of kickboxing, another on the road before him. In the safe neighborhood of the Elite Compound, he had not a worry in the world.

The *War of Sovereign Nations* game had left him feeling pleased with himself and yet at the same time vaguely disappointed. *Such a sick idea to play that way, they never saw it coming.*

The large mansions were illuminated; the street before him was immaculate and well-manicured. He would be home shortly, where he lived with his dad.

Suddenly, he felt a crushing blow to his head. He fell down and a succession of rapid kicks to his ribs and head caused him to writhe in pain, and finally sank him into darkness. Sometime later, he woke up for a brief moment to the sound of an ambulance, and then promptly lost consciousness again.

2

Jules was a Scrappie, a runaway Server. For three months, she had been living in the Scrappie Compound in an old house, repaired and inhabited by Tom, the tall, middle aged man who had found her half frozen in the forest and taken her into his home and heart. He soon became like the father she never knew.

She was sixteen, yet felt worn out, her whole world a terrible burden to be carried each day. She needed to work to support herself and her new family of sorts, and thus she had to pretend she was still a Server, even though she had run away from her abusive home. She had her old ID card and the fact that nobody had declared her gone helped keep her somewhat legitimate.

Coming out of the forest, she left behind the shade of the trees, and even farther away, the tall buildings in ruin, where the Scrappies lived. She moved towards a long row of apartment buildings in the Server Compound. From a shed nearby, she retrieved her red e-bike, the paint chipping on the sides. She put on a helmet hanging from the handle and climbed on the bike.

She was wearing a worn-out yellow T-shirt and blue jeans, black running shoes and a backpack, nothing ripped or stained; her blonde hair tied neatly in the back.

Jules could see the sun setting over the water as she crossed Golden Bridge, which separated the compound where most of the Servers lived from the other areas of the city. Soon the sun would disappear beyond the fog. She stopped for a moment.

Beautiful. Like magic come to life. A symphony of colors surrounded the setting sun. At this time of the day, everything seemed right in the world. Jules allowed herself a few moments of daydreaming. Reflections of the large Elite mansions trembled on the silvery waters of the wide canal. *How would my life be if I were one of them? It must feel great to be rich and spoiled, to have friends I could meet at school, to feel safe, most of all.* The reality of her own life brought up the inevitable question. *What future will I have? There's no future for me…*

It was getting late. She made an effort to dismiss the fear gripping her heart and started again in the direction of the hospital, where she worked a couple of times each week, just a few hours a day. With so many Servers around, she was lucky to have a job, as menial as it was. There was no point in dreaming of what she couldn't possibly have, and no point in worrying over what she could not control.

By the time she reached the Professionals' compound, the street lights had already been turned on and the light was creating ethereal shadows of her body and the bike. They alternated; short, long, longer, disappearing and being re-created as she rode on. The houses on both sides of the road were large and well maintained – raised ranch houses with cathedral ceilings and chandeliers visible from the outside through the tall glass entrances. The trees were relatively small and widely spaced and the lawns looked freshly cut.

She could feel her pulse like a fast drumbeat under her skin and she realized she was scared, but she tried to convince herself there was no reason for her fear. *No need to hide, I have an ID card to prove I belong here in the city.*

The street was empty. Everybody was at home by now, watching their wall-sized digiscreens as they had their supper. A slim, middle aged woman in gym clothes had just turned the corner and was jogging towards her. She had hyper-goggles over her eyes so she could watch a hypernet show while still keeping an eye on her surroundings.

As Jules neared the hospital she could see an ambulance approaching fast, sirens blaring and lights blinking. An emergency was in progress. She wondered idly who was hurt and how it had happened. One thing was for sure: in this hospital only the Elites and the Professionals were admitted.

Walking her e-bike towards the side parking lot, she couldn't help but see the stretcher being pushed through the sliding doors by two paramedics. On the stretcher, a young face was streaked with blood and dirt. The head was turned sideways towards her and she was struck with unimaginable sorrow for the young man. He opened his eyes and kept them on her even as they were moving him away.

Please don't die! Don't do this to me! Jules felt the horror as strongly as ever, fearing she would once again play an active role in the replacement of yet another human.

~~~

Siren noises woke him up again. Allan opened his eyes this time and saw strange faces looking at him with concern in their eyes. "Stay still," a woman was saying as she leaned down towards him. "You'll be fine."

She placed a mask over his mouth and gently lifted him to stretch the elastic band around the back of his head. He could breathe easier immediately, but something was wrong. He couldn't feel his body. He tried to move a finger, then a toe. Nothing.

Allan was moved to a stretcher and people were rushing and pushing him towards the ER entrance. His head was leaning on the side and he felt utterly helpless as he tried to form a word. He couldn't even move his lips. *What's wrong with me?* He wanted to scream. Only his eyes were able to move and he scanned the perimeter bathed in electric lights.

He saw a girl by her e-bike, standing nearby with a hand over her mouth, looking at him. Her eyes were frightened and sad. He kept looking at her until they moved him past the sliding door of the emergency area, and she was gone from view.

Then everything happened very fast. Allan could not seem to think straight; a sheer terror at what was going to happen next gripped him. He heard someone say, "Bring him in here." The stretcher was pushed into a large, immaculate room with a bright light emanating from the entire ceiling. Anti-gravity forces generated by the gravitron placed straight overhead lifted him up and placed him on a white block with cables and hoses and all kinds of instruments protruding from the sides. This was the operating cube. Allan ended up on his stomach, with his head tilted to one side.

"Is the C here yet?" the same voice asked.

"Almost here. Is this really necessary, doctor?" a younger woman's voice questioned.

"Yes. Put him under now."

A man in a blue operating gown was standing beside him. Allan couldn't see his face, but he could smell an expensive musky fragrance coming from him. "Do not worry, dear boy, you'll be fine when you wake up," the surgeon was saying softly. His eyelids started to close and he sank into oblivion.

Allan regained consciousness slowly. With great effort he managed to open his eyes, and discovered that he was on his back, with his head leaning to the side. For a moment he was confused. Lying on another cube directly opposite him, he saw another man, one who looked exactly like him. *It is C.* The realization that he was being discarded began to sink in. Terror enveloped him. He tried to get up but was unable to do so. He simply could not feel his body.

His eyes filled with tears and he hoped someone would see them running over the base of his nose and realize he was not dead. Then he reasoned that they must have known that already because they had instruments monitoring his vitals. The only conclusion he could conjure was that the decision had already been made to have him replaced. The thought of his father doing that to him was unbearable. *Surely it's a mistake, it must be a mistake.* Before he could ponder on this any longer, he saw some movement at the corner of his eye, green coveralls, and knew that his time was up. A few seconds later his world darkened into nothingness.

3

After seeing the stretcher pushed inside the ER reception area, Jules made her way towards Floor 2, which housed the Recovery wing, where her assignment would begin shortly. Her job tonight was to empty and wash all the bed pans, then remove the containers with bloody bandages and take them to the incinerator. After that she had to take the soiled hospital gowns and have them placed in the chutes to be recycled. More tasks of that nature would follow.

From the janitorial closet she grabbed a pair of coveralls, shoe covers, nitrile gloves, and a hair net. She put them on and then attached a face mask over her mouth. The hospital maintained strict regulations so the Servers wouldn't contaminate the hyper clean environment, including the expensive medical creams and powders. She also knew it was for her own protection. Most of those substances contained nanobots specialized in so many different ways that one never knew what they were going to do upon contact with the skin. Nanobots could enter her body through just a simple scratch.

An hour or so into work, Emma, the floor head nurse, approached her. She was tall and willowy, bald headed, with green eyes matching her jumpsuit and goggles. "Julia, they need you in the OR now. Take the cleaning unit with you."

Sensing the note of urgency in Emma's voice, Jules rushed with the cleaning cart via the closest elevator to the operating room. Once inside, she saw the bodies of two young men laid down on two operating cubes. They were identical, except that one was bruised and bloody, the other immaculately clean and beautiful like a marble sculpture. *It's the man from the ambulance. He didn't make it.* She felt a sudden sadness. The other one was surely his clone.

Jules could see they both had headsets on, forming the pathway for memory transfer from one to the other. Magnetic nanobots in both brains, once activated, clustered and acted as an interface between their synapses.

A nurse with a mask on was signaling her to approach. "Wipe the mess from the floor, then take the body from here to the incinerator as soon as I'm done with it and I move it to the stretcher. Hurry up, the father will be here any minute to see his son."

Obviously not his original son. She bit her tongue to stop herself from saying something she'd regret.

She proceeded to clean the floor as fast as possible, her entire focus on the task at hand. She was careful and efficient, cleaning as thoroughly as possible to assure future jobs here. In the meantime, the man to be discarded was being transported to the stretcher by invisible hands, as if levitating. She stole a glance at him: he looked like a fallen angel, a slim, bruised body floating through the air.

Once she finished with the floors, she put the cleaning unit away and went to the stretcher. The dead man was lying on his back, his dark locks falling over his bruised face, eyes closed as if asleep. He looked peaceful and handsome, Jules observed, tracing with her eyes his square jawline and dimpled chin, moving towards his full lips and straight-edged nose. *What a pity! All his dreams shattered.* Then she realized they were able to copy his memory onto the clone after all, given the nurse's remarks.

She began to wonder if the clone would just wake up and resume his existence like the original, as if nothing has changed at all. *They say that's true, but how can that be? What happens to the soul?* There was so much thinking and feeling inside her, she couldn't imagine her essence being captured by a computer program.

She placed a cover on the body and started pushing it out of the room. *How many times have I done this?* She counted six or seven. It never got any easier, no matter how many times she did it, seeing how Elites were disposed of so casually. Who else could afford to keep one or two bodies around, just in case? *But are they sure it's truly their own self coming back to life?* No one had ever said any differently.

The incinerator was in the basement. After exiting the maintenance elevator, she pushed the stretcher slowly, feeling like she could somehow delay the inevitable. Everything was done through the back corridors. "No need to show our patients or visitors the unpleasant side of the business, Julia," Emma had told her once. She opened the door to the incinerator and pushed the button to pneumatically lift one side of the stretcher.

All of a sudden Jules saw some movement underneath the cover, and it looked like the blanket came to life, lifting and sliding away. On the stretcher, the young man was lowering one arm, having let go of the discarded cover, face up and eyes looking pleadingly at her.

"You are alive!" she exclaimed, hands shaking in shock. Her knees became wobbly.

He stared at her. His lips moved but no words came out.

She pulled the stretcher away from the incinerator and hurried to the other side of it so she could face him and, afraid that somebody might catch them, blurted out, "I was supposed to take you away and incinerate you. You were badly damaged and a clone is probably talking to your father right now. You do not exist anymore, do you understand me?"

He looked in her eyes for a few seconds, the situation sinking in for him, and he nodded. He understood.

"What do you want me to do?" she asked, at a loss for a solution.

His eyes were filling with tears, he was scared or lost, she didn't know. His lips moved again and she heard a whisper, "Bad?"

"You mean how badly you were injured?" She looked at his body, trying hard to avoid her sudden embarrassment at seeing him naked. "Some swelling in the ribs area, head bloody, bruises all over. Can you feel your body?"

He nodded yes.

"Then you might have a chance to recover, unless there are some massive internal injuries I cannot see," she added. *Why would they discard an able human being? And did they forget to inject him with the deadly serum? Or they didn't care...* Her mind raced as she forced herself to come back to the pressing issue at hand. "I don't know what to do. Do you want me to call somebody to come take you away?"

He thought for a few seconds and shook his head in negation.

"What, then? You have any idea?"

A jagged whisper came out of his mouth, "Away."

"You want *me* to take you away?" she asked incredulously.

He nodded yes.

"You don't understand. Where can I take you? I'm not actually a valid Server, I'm —"She lowered her voice to a whisper. "I'm a Scrappie. We can't possibly get to where I live in your condition. It's too dangerous for both of us. Besides, you need medical care. You'd be better off with a friend or family member." She was out of breath and felt totally overwhelmed.

"Away," he whispered again.

She could see the fear in his eyes. Who could blame him? He would be discarded, killed, simply because someone else had already taken his place in the world. He was supposed to be ashes by now. She had to decide. Either take charge of him or let somebody at the hospital know of the situation.

Before she could decide what to do, the door opened and a man in blue overalls, pushing a container on wheels, came in.

"Oh, Bruce, it's you!" she exclaimed. "You scared me out of my skin."

The utility man was an older, stocky guy who always had a smile on his round face and a gentle manner. He stopped, swept the room with his baby-blue watery eyes and seemed to have grasped the truth immediately.

"How come he's alive?" he asked.

"I don't know. They brought him to Emergency, had his memory copied to the C, and I was just carrying him here to… you know…" she pointed to the incinerator. "And he woke up."

"And just what were you going to do with him?"

"I don't know. Help, if possible. What *can* I do?"

He shook his head disapprovingly. "My dear Jules, this is trouble. Nobody is allowed to walk away."

Jules felt torn apart between the desire to save that man and the horror of being caught and taken to the Happy Endings clinic. *Oh, God, what can I do? If somebody finds out what I am doing, I'm history. But how can I let this human being be put to death?* But then, maybe they wouldn't put him to death when they found out he's not dead. What if she was wrong? She remembered how only hours earlier she had thought she had no future anyway. What difference would it make if they caught her now or later? At least she could save someone's life.

Jules' mind worked frenetically to come up with a solution. The man was an Elite, therefore his body could speed up the recovery. She had seen it happen with the Elites in the hospital. If she could just take him away from there and hide him for a while, until he would be able to move. All of a sudden an idea popped up on her mind. "The utility vehicle! Let's get him inside and then you can drop us at the forest. I'll take it from there."

Bruce scratched his chin in doubt. "Jules, that's madness. We'll be caught and that will be the end of us. Get a hold of yourself, and let the nurse know what happened here. That's for the best, sweetie."

"I can't do that to him, Bruce," she pleaded with the older man. "Think how you'll feel in the future knowing you could have saved somebody and yet you chose not to do anything at all? Think Bruce, what a difference you made in my life. Without you, I'd probably be out there being hunted down, or I would have killed myself. But you helped me once, in fact, more than once. Do it again, please Bruce? Help me save this one." Her tears flowed freely as she talked, every second making the difference between life and death to that young man.

Bruce gave her a long look, seemingly trying to weigh the options. Their eyes met and the desperate plea of her eyes reached his soul, beyond all the words she could have uttered. "What the heck, let's do it. For you, my darling Jules, one more time," he agreed in a shaky voice, obviously deeply touched.

She ran to him and hugged him fiercely, catching him off guard. "Thank you, Bruce!"

"The best way to take him out is with these used sheets." He pointed to the container beside the door. "It's easier to hide him on the way to the vehicle." It seemed like an excellent idea, she agreed.

"Hang on," Jules said to the young man, as she moved to the stretcher and looked at his frightened eyes. "Soon we'll be out of here. I'll be back for you."

The rest happened in a blur. They moved the young man carefully into the box among the uniforms and Bruce pushed it outside, but not before they planned where to meet after the shift was over.

Back on the second floor, Emma sat at her station with her hyper-goggles on her eyes. She gave Jules a casual glance, obviously watching something on the hypernet or remotely checking on a patient, "Everything in order, Julia?"

"Yes, of course." The answer came shakily; she hoped Emma would not observe her distress. "Everything went as expected."

"Go on then, and hurry up. The pans are overflowing."

Close to midnight, Jules finished her work, hurrying downstairs to change her clothes and leave the hospital. As she rode away on her e-bike, she heard Bruce start the van. In a darkened street a short distance from the hospital, she found the van waiting and together they traveled to the Servers' compound. Bruce drove around to the back of the row of buildings. She placed her e-bike back in the shed and plugged it in to be recharged, while he backed the utility vehicle towards the forest. Together they carried the young man and placed him on the ground behind a tree, farther away from the forest's edge, cocooned in a blanket Bruce took from the van.

"Goodbye, my girl," Bruce said. "And good luck to you both." She hugged him and he walked away, got into the van, and headed back to the hospital.

Jules slid down against the tree. "What a scare! I never thought I would be doing this in a million years."

They looked at each other in silence for a while, eyes wide with an air of total exhaustion around them.

"Are you comfortable? Anything else I can do for you?" she asked, her hand reaching to touch his forehead and re-arrange a rebel lock of hair spread on his face.

He just smiled with a sigh.

She sighed and closed her eyes. "Let's rest for a while. I hope you'll recover somewhat by morning. Then we'll decide what to do." The exhaustion enveloped her and before she finished her thought, she was asleep.

4

The sound of birds chirping woke Allan up. His first reaction was one of utter confusion. Where was he? Then he remembered his close encounter with death the night before.

He opened his eyes and saw tree branches hovering over him. He felt chilly in spite of the blanket around him, and was suddenly afraid he was still critically wounded. *Nothing hurts, that's a good sign.* He attempted a stretch of his body, and he was happy beyond belief when he succeeded without major pain, only some discomfort in the rib area and a dull headache.

Man, it feels good. I'll be all right. He pushed his body up with his palms on the ground. Then he slowly stood up, trying to overcome an unexpected light headed sensation. He stretched once more, his arms reaching over his head and his feet apart, firmly planted on the ground. *Alive and reasonably well, thank goodness!* He felt chilled to the bone, naked as he was, so he took the blanket from the ground and placed it around his shoulders.

Allan saw the girl who had helped him sleeping on her side in the fetal position, probably trying to keep her warm breath close to her body and limbs. She looked so vulnerable, so graceful in her sleep. *What was her name?*

He tried to remember. *Jules. The man had called her Jules. Well, thank you Jules, for saving me.* The sight of her filled him with gratitude. He realized she must feel cold and looked around for something to cover her with. Then he remembered his blanket. He had nothing on underneath, but figured it was the least he could do for her. He took the blanket from his shoulders and gently placed it on her.

Tidal waves of troubling thoughts reached him suddenly, and in order to fight the settling panic, he decided to do something to clear his mind. He began with a tai-chi routine, which filled him with energy through fluidic movements and breathing patterns. *Breathe in, feel light as the clouds, breath out, and feel heavy as the mountain.* After a few minutes, he felt his body and mind invigorated and ready for the tremendous challenges ahead.

What now? He knew instinctively he should go home and straighten things out. Some terrible mistake had happened. His father would be able to help him. Allan was sure he was totally unaware of what had happened. *How could he not know?* He suddenly felt lost and scared. *I thought tai-chi would help clear my mind. What a mess!* He tried to cheer himself up. *I'm alive.* That was definitely a good thing. There must be an explanation. He just needed to get some clothes with Jules' help and go straight home, where he belonged.

Allan saw some movement from Jules' direction. She was waking up. He moved towards her. He thought all of a sudden of his nakedness, and for a moment he couldn't think what to do to make himself presentable. He had a sudden idea, and he knelt down in front of Jules with his hands in front of his body.

Jules was still lying at the base of the tree and was stretching under the blanket. She opened her eyes and looked at him, a hint of fear on her face.

"It's high time you wake up, sleeping beauty," Allan remarked cheerfully, feeling slightly embarrassed by his choice of words. *Sleeping Beauty, seriously?*

"Are you kidding me?" she replied, feisty even though barely awake. "Last night you were dying and now you're teasing me?"

"No reason to be in a bad mood," Allan put on a good-humored face. "The fact that I am alive after last night's scare is nothing short of a miracle. Besides, I'm terribly hungry. By the way, I'm Allan," he said, putting out his hand. "And you are Jules, as I learned last night."

"They call me Julia in the city, but I'm Jules to friends," she explained. "How are you even up so soon? Last night you were a complete mess." She sat up and moved away from his face, offering the blanket back to him. The closeness appeared to make her uncomfortable.

"The nanobots did their job," he answered, taking the blanket and trying to cover his nakedness.

"I forgot you're an Elite. The *privileged* class and all," she replied, standing up.

"Was that sarcasm? Anyway, that's just how my body was equipped, with enhanced natural abilities to heal," Allan continued, wrapping the blanket around his body. "It's rather chilly to be naked in the woods at this time of day." He looked at her with a sheepish look in his eyes. "Do you think you could help me get some clothes so I can go back home?"

"So you want to go home now? After they *killed you*?" She drew quotes with her hands.

"What else would you suggest?"

"I suggest you take some time to think about what happened to you last night and think about all your options before you rush head first to your next untimely death."

What's wrong with her? Allan was puzzled by Jules' aggressive reaction to everything he said.

Suddenly he remembered. "By the way, I forgot to thank you from the bottom of my heart for saving me. And I truly mean it."

Jules just glanced back in his direction and started to wipe away the leaves and grass from her clothes.

"You know," he said after a moment of silence. "I think you're right. There *was* something odd going on. Maybe I should go to one of my friends."

She shook her head, as if his agreeing with her wasn't acceptable either. "Tell you what. You might be healed physically, but I think your mind still needs some mending. It's dangerous to stay here any longer. Why don't you tear two pieces off this blanket and wrap them over your feet? Then wrap the rest of the blanket around yourself. We'll go to my place. It's time for you to meet my friends and get some advice from them. Oh, and thank you for covering me up last night."

"You're welcome," he felt his lips curling up in a tiny smile, too embarrassed to admit that he had covered her only minutes earlier. "I'll follow your lead then." He started ripping the blanket.

They entered the forest, leaving the city behind, and walked under the canopy of trees. Dead branches and last year's leaves abundantly covered the ground. It was obvious that people took care of areas close to the city but nobody bothered to clean up further away. Jules walked in front, following an almost invisible path that started somewhere inside the forest.

She asked Allan about the details of his ordeal, and he was glad to be able to order his thoughts as he expressed them out loud. There was not much to be said, though, and he soon found himself again at a loss of understanding what had happened. He asked for her opinion, but she couldn't come up with an explanation either. They continued their journey through the forest.

"Is it far, where we're going?" Allan was curious, avoiding sharp stumps that could hurt his wrapped feet.

"About three miles," Jules replied without turning her head.

"I've never been out here before. Is it safe?"

She turned her head, glancing at him. "Safer than the city; for me, anyway."

"How far have you gone?"

"Just as far as the lake, on the other side of downtown."

"Downtown?"

"That is what they used to call this place. That was before the great quake." She was silent for a while, as if she was thinking of the tragedy.

"I know about the quake," Allan remembered the stories his father had told him, which filled him with deep sadness. "More than two million people died back then. Most of the high risers were badly damaged. But there's no point in fixing them, is there?"

"I guess not," she replied absently. She didn't speak again until they'd reached the other side of the forest. "We're two miles away now."

They both stopped for a moment, side by side, to look at the landscape. In front of them there were one and two-story houses in varying stages of decay. They were lined up in rows like spokes of a wheel leading to tall structures in the distance, derelict skyscrapers towering over the buildings like a gaping mouth.

Here and there, several people dressed in shaggy clothes were moving around, in and out of the decrepit buildings, carrying various items; a chair, a pot, all kinds of things that could be of some use.

"What is this place?" Allan asked, looking at her.

"This is the Scrappie neighborhood, the place where you will be able to work on your *plan*," she answered with a smirk, as she emphasized the last word.

"Your sarcasm is getting on my nerves."

"I'm sorry, I can't help it. I'm not what one would call the biggest fan of the Elites," she confessed, seemingly embarrassed at her unexpected aggression. "But I wanted to help you, somehow. And I still want to."

"Why do you hate us?"

"You have it all just because you won the womb lottery."

"What do you mean?"

"You came out of an Elite woman's womb. Born rich and privileged, while all the rest of us are struggling." Her face was getting red in sudden anger.

"Actually, I was born in-vitro."

"Whatever," she turned her eyes to the view in front of them.

Together they stepped into the crisp light of the morning sun and entered the compound.

Allan felt a slight fear gripping his heart. Had he escaped one danger only to step into a worse one? *This place is creepy. Can I trust Jules?* He admitted to himself that she could be part of the plot that landed him in this situation in the first place. He vowed that if he was attacked again, he wouldn't go down without a fight. He started to look closely at the people they encountered. Some of them gave him curious glances, but then they resumed their scavenging activities. Allan started to feel curiosity more than danger.

"What are these people doing?" he asked.

"They're shopping," Jules answered. "Whenever someone needs something, they go and look for that particular item in the old houses. There's still a lot of stuff there; a plate, a cup, a pot, a table and so on. Some of the people you see are newcomers to the Scrappie compound, others are in need of a replacement for something that broke. Their needs are many."

"Do they live in these houses? Some of them are falling apart, literally."

"Most of the Scrappies live closer to downtown. They fixed those buildings the best they could. They like to keep an additional buffer between themselves and the city, in case someone ventures to this side of the forest. Nobody wants to be the first to be seen and taken. The farther away, the better." Jules let off a deep sigh, and added, "Still not far enough for me..."

5

After walking through a couple of blocks of decrepit buildings, they turned a corner and found themselves in front of a small weather-beaten looking house covered with brown bricks and climbing plants in the front. A fenced yard surrounded the sides, continuing towards the back of the house. In the front, a few chickens were running around chasing each other for a worm one of them had plucked from a hole in the dirt.

The scene was so unexpected; Allan let a small laugh escape his mouth.

He gestured at the chickens. "Is this the welcoming committee?"

With the hint of a smile, Jules opened the gates and walked towards the house. Allan followed her. The chickens stopped suddenly, moving their heads sideways to look at them curiously for a moment, then resumed their chase.

"I'm home!" Jules announced loudly as they entered.

"Good, 'cause it's your turn to milk the goats," a voice answered. A slim, dark haired girl with her hair braided in two pigtails ran down the stairs facing the front door. She was wearing a long, flowery skirt down to her ankles and a white peasant blouse.

"Goats...?" Allan echoed as he entered the house.

"His name is not Goats, it's Allan. And this is Mel." Jules made the introduction with a smirk on her face.

"Right. And why did you bring him here?" Mel asked with a frown on her face.

"It's a long story. He needs to figure some things out for himself."

Mel lowered her voice, thinking only Jules could hear. "You know what Tom said. No strangers in our home."

"No worries," Jules continued in a normal voice. "He'll be gone soon." She turned towards Allan. "Let's go upstairs so you can get cleaned and dressed. There's a collection of clothes and shoes you can look through." She looked him up and down, his body covered sparingly with the blanket. "Hopefully some will fit you."

~~~

They returned downstairs to find a young man, his blond hair in a ponytail, dressed in black track pants and a grey t-shirt, sitting at a table by the window. He was slouched over a book, eating scrambled eggs.

"Hi, Daniel!" Jules greeted her friend and took a seat at the table, one hand gesturing at Allan to do the same.

"You're late. I was worried about you." He looked at Allan. "Picking up strays again?"

"Daniel, this is Allan, a friend. Allan, meet Daniel, our scientist in residence." Jules started picking scrambled eggs from Daniel's plate and placing them in her mouth.

"How many times have I told you to keep away from my plate?" Daniel mumbled, his mouth full.

"But you always cook the most delicious food. Is there any left for us?"

"Sure. On the stove," he pointed with his head. "What's up, man?" he asked Allan.

"I needed some help and Jules offered to take me in."

"She does that a lot. She did that to me, a while back."

"And look what happened. Now we're stuck with you," Jules smiled, chewing the food she had retrieved from the stove. Looking at Allan, she said, "If you want to eat or whatever, just help yourself. We're rather casual around here."

"All right, thanks. And thanks for the clothes, Daniel. Hope you don't mind I raided your closet."

"No problem, man," Daniel responded, his head bent over the book he'd resumed reading.

They ate together, while Jules described briefly to Daniel the sequence of events that led to Allan's rescue. She finished her breakfast in a hurry and rushed outside to the back of the house to do her chores. Allan found himself alone with Daniel and wondered at the lack of interest on the young man's part, who seemed oblivious to the world around him. He decided to try making conversation to try to find out more about his new acquaintance.

"So you really are a researcher," Allan remarked.

"No, I'm not. Not anymore," Daniel lifted his eyes from the book and placed it aside.

"Why, what happened?"

"I got burnt out and left, came here to live with the Scrappies." Daniel kept his eyes on the table, in a reflective state of mind, as if trying to find the right words, and continued. "It feels good, you know? Feels wholesome, like life makes sense when you take pleasure in simple things and live close to nature. Planting something in a garden for example, then picking the veggies or the fruits and eating them right then and there. We are screwed up when we sell our conscience for material wealth." He stretched his back and looked at Allan, as if seeing him for the first time. "So what's your story, man?"

"I don't know exactly. Still trying to figure it out..." Allan debated how much he should tell a new acquaintance, then made up his mind. "One instant I was walking home, tired and satisfied after winning a new game at the Imaginarium, and the next thing I know I'm staring at a clone who was ready to take my whole life from me. I still can't figure out what happened."

"Were you in an accident?"

"Not really. It was an attack. Someone knocked me down from behind. They kicked me pretty badly. Luckily, I heal fast. An ambulance took me to the hospital and Jules told you what happened there. She took me to the incinerator, except I wasn't dead. She saved my life." Allan paused for a moment, suddenly lost in thought. "Why do you think I'm here? Why switch us, the clone and me? My father was on his way to see me. Why didn't they wait for him to see me before putting me down? Obviously I wasn't critically injured."

"Indeed, why?" Daniel looked intently at Allan, his green eyes partially closed, eyelids heavy with long lashes that made him look sleepy. "What generation was your clone?"

"C5, I think. Why?"

"Just curious. At the very least you can rest assured he's going to be very much like you. A lot of the psychological and emotional issues were debugged in the C5s. Their synapses connect much faster and with greater accuracy. He'll be You in no time."

"Were you a geneticist?"

"Ph.D. in stem cell transplant, but I worked a lot with cloned material, used it for organ replacement and such. I worked at the cloning lab, too, for a while. Might have seen You there," he winked. "What's your specialty?"

"My father is the head of Secure-IT. I was lined up to take his place one day and so all my education and training are in security systems and technology, hardware, a bit of software." He paused. "And combat," Allan added finally.

"That didn't help you much in a street fight," Daniel teased him.

"You're right, but I didn't see it coming. I'm not trying to make excuses or anything, but I was listening to music, watching some game and walking in a safe zone. I was tired too, the Imaginarium thing, you know."

"The lesson is to watch your back. Be on constant alert from now on, even here with the Scrappies. There is no safe haven for you, my friend; for none of us."

"Speaking of which, Mel was telling Jules about a Tom who said no strangers in the house. Who is he?"

"Tom is our host. He took Jules in to live here with him. Mel came next, brought in by Jules. I was the last one Jules found. Tom agreed to let us all stay here. The other Scrappies respect him or are afraid of him, not sure which, but they leave us alone. They don't try to steal anything from us or take over the house."

"Where is he now?" Allan asked.

"He comes and goes. We don't know his whereabouts. Sometimes he goes back into town and brings us food or medicine, things that we need to survive. He's like a father to us all. He even helps some of the other groups from other houses with critical needs; a child being sick, some hot heads fighting over something or another. He likes it peaceful around here, so he gets involved to keep some sort of order."

"Is he a Scrappie?"

"Definitely. He's in hiding from something but again, we don't know the details. Some of us think he was an Elite or Professional by the way he talks and holds himself; a person used to being in charge." Daniel continued appraising him. "You look a bit like him, you know?"

"Do you think I could talk to him and get some advice?"

"Sure thing. You just have to wait for him to come home. Sometimes he stays away for days."

"What would you do, if you were me?"

"If I were you, I'd stay put for a while and see what happens."

"What else could happen? Some clone stole my whole life away and lives as *me*. I think I have to confront him and clear things up with my father."

"Well, apparently you already know the answer to your question. That's a tough call, and it's your decision." Daniel got up and started towards the back door. "Let's go outside and see if we can help."

Allan followed, his frustration increasing. *These people don't know any more than I do what the best course of action is. I'm just wasting my time with them.*

The back of the house was full of activity. Birds up in the trees called to one another. A baby goat jumped up and down near its mother, who was trying to reach some leaves just outside the fence. Jules began chasing after another goat, its udder swollen with milk, while Mel was feeding the chickens that were stepping on her sandals in a joyful flutter – breakfast at last!

"This is awesome!" Allan exclaimed, taking in the whole scene. After a short glance at Daniel, who was shaking his head with a smile on his face, he went to help Jules.

After helping with the animals, Allan felt very weak and light headed. "I think I need to rest for a bit. I suppose my body is still in recovery mode," he told Jules.

"I thought you recovered extremely well," Jules remarked. "Go upstairs and rest for a while. You'll feel much better. Then we can talk about your *strategy*," she ended with a grin.

"You really can't help yourself, can you?" Allan replied, looking at her, then he addressed them all. "I'll go inside for a nap. See you later, and thank you all for everything."

6

Allan woke up to noise coming from downstairs. His stomach was rumbling with hunger, so he got up to join the others. His mind was made up: he was going home, where *he* belonged, not a freaky clone.

He looked outside through the window. The afternoon sun had turned the backyard into a deserted place. All the animals were hiding in the shade. Everybody was probably inside the house where the air conditioner, taking its energy from the sun itself, as he had found out, was maintaining a welcoming ambience.

Allan headed downstairs and found Jules, Mel, and Daniel in the living room, each of them engaged in a different activity; Daniel reading, Mel mending some clothes, Jules arranging flowers in a vase.

"Oh, you're up. Feeling better?" Jules inquired.

"Much better, thanks," Allan replied.

"When is David coming?" Jules addressed Daniel.

"Speaking of the devil?" a young man said, entering the house. He dropped the backpack he had been carrying to the floor. He was a shorter version of his brother Daniel, but livelier. His dirty blond hair was cut short and his green eyes sparkled with mischief, seemingly ready for a hot debate on any topic. "What's up, dudes? I see I'm not the only visitor," he continued, looking at Allan while lowering himself on the couch.

"Jules brought in a man she rescued at the hospital. His name is Allan." Mel leaned over and whispered loudly, "He's an Elite."

"Allan, this is David, Daniel's brother," Jules intervened.

"Good to meet you, man," Allan said, and the two young men shook hands.

"What happened to you?" David asked, with apparent concern in his voice.

Allan repeated the story he had told Daniel. "So, now I need to straighten everything out. Do you guys have any advice for me?" he finished, looking at each of them in turn.

Nobody volunteered an answer, waiting for David to give them his opinion.

"It's hard to say. I haven't heard of anything like this happening before. Do you have any other relatives you can count on?"

"Nobody else, except my father. Mother died a long time ago, so did my grandparents, and I am an only child."

"Do you trust your father?" David continued questioning Allan.

"With my life. I have no idea whatsoever why things turned out this way. There is no reasonable explanation."

"Have you considered that your father might be the target, and you just a casualty?"

"Not really, but since you mention it, he has seemed preoccupied lately. A bit distant, but he hasn't said anything to me, so I don't know what it could be."

"Then I would go and confront him about it. What do you guys think?" David looked at the others.

"He could wait for a few days, to see if something else happens," Daniel reflected. "The problem right now is that he is too far removed to see anything. At times like this, one would like to be a fly on the wall, present but unnoticeable."

Jules had kept her silence up to that point, but she seemed to have remembered something. "There was something in that nurse's tone of voice, rushing me to take Allan away, saying it was because the father was coming to see his son. I don't think Allan's father was aware of the change and was rushing to see what he thought to be his original son, who had been in an accident. What if the guys at the hospital were doing the replacement without his father's knowledge or consent?"

"Why would the hospital want to have me replaced?" Allan felt fear gripping his heart. "The more I think about what happened, the worse I feel. I have to talk to my father."

"All right. The decision rests with you," David seemed relieved to not make the decision for Allan. "What's Tom saying about the whole story?"

"He hasn't heard it. We don't know where he is at the moment," Mel replied.

"Don't you want to wait and see what he has to say? He has sound judgment." David asked.

"What could he tell me that I don't already know? I'm in trouble and I have to face whatever is that wants me dead."

"Let's see, then, today is Friday," he looked down at his watch. "It's getting late and I have some errands to do in town. How about I take you home tomorrow morning? It's less conspicuous during the day to walk in and out of the Elite compound, and besides, your face still looks a bit rugged. A few more hours of nano-healing would help with your bruises. Is your father usually home on Saturday morning?"

"Yes, he is," Allan confirmed.

"Sounds like a plan, then?" David asked, looking at them all to see if they objected.

"Agreed," Allan said. "That is, if they'll have me." He looked at the others, hoping they would let him stay with them a bit longer.

"I have no problem, under the condition you leave tomorrow. We'll be in danger with you here if it turns out they discover you didn't die at the hospital after all," Jules said, expressing the fear they all apparently felt.

"But we'll do our best to help you as much as we can," Mel added softly.

"And, man, don't be a fool. Despite what Jules said, if something goes wrong, just come back. We'll be here," Daniel finished.

"I'll do that. So, what's for dinner?" Allan asked, the noise in his stomach a clear indication of his most immediate concern.

"I forgot you slept through lunch," Jules exclaimed. "Mel, we have a hungry man in the house!"

"Two hungry men, truth be told," David added. "I have some rice in the backpack, if you want to add that to the stew I'm sniffing."

Over dinner, they made some casual conversation. Allan was interested to find out more about the two brothers, especially about Daniel's choice of giving up his future. "So you're with the Professionals," he started, looking at David.

"Always have been. I'm a computer science major. From time to time, I come to visit my brother. Mom and dad are still devastated because he ran away. They had great expectations from him. I keep hoping one day he'll come back home with me."

"Not going to happen," Daniel's tone was decisive. "Done too much, seen too many awful things out there in my profession. I've done my share of work for this "beautiful" world." He seemed deeply wounded and all their eyes moved to him.

"What happened to you there?" Allan asked, curious.

"You don't know what they were doing to the clones. We killed young babies just because they weren't matching the design specs. We harvested them for their organs when their original was in surgery. I just wanted to work strictly in my field. But it was never enough for them."

"For who?" Allan asked with interest.

"All those hot shots at the institute and the associated cloning lab, "Why don't you try to expand your limits, Daniel? Why not use your exceptional qualities to achieve more? Why limit yourself to lab work, you and your microscope?" I tried again and again to tell them it was too much for me. I was having nightmares, dreaming of all those poor kids suddenly transformed into zombies, coming after me. Ultimately, I lost it and ran as far as I could," he finished with an exhausted breath.

"It's over now, Daniel," Mel tried to comfort him, getting up from the couch and sitting beside him. "We all have our nightmares, but we have each other to watch our backs now. And Allan, will you stop prying? It's not good for him to talk about it."

"Hey," intervened David. "Allan didn't know he would bring up such memories. Take it easy, brother, there's no hurry to do anything."

Allan suddenly felt very sorry for Daniel. "Look man, I didn't mean to upset you. I'm truly sorry. I've had it easy my whole life, I can see that now. I can promise you one thing: if I don't end up dead, I will do everything in my power to make a difference in people's lives. Nobody should ever have to go through what you or I did."

"Oh, Allan, you're so full of it," Jules replied in a bitter tone. "You'll just end up enjoying your life once again and forgetting that this ever happened to you."

"I'm really starting to wonder why you even bothered to save me if you think so little of me!" Allan felt a rush of contradictory emotions engulfing his being. "I was simply oblivious to what was happening in the world. All the other young Elites are just like me, but I can assure you I will never be the same, knowing what I know now. Give me a chance to prove myself before you rush to conclusions." He stormed outside, all the while feeling the inadequacy of his words, especially coming from somebody not even in control of his own destiny.

Mel followed him and looked at him with sympathy. Then she said, "Please don't blame Jules. It's so much better to say what you think than to keep it all bottled up. Don't you see how good it is to see us, all from different classes, opening up in front of each other, on equal footing? At least here we can start anew, being totally ourselves with all our strengths and weaknesses. This is truly the beginning of genuine friendship. I wish you could see just how special she is. She doesn't hate you, Allan, she hates the system. But she saved us all, even risked her life, as in your case. Let's just enjoy an evening of friendship and we'll see what tomorrow brings."

7

Allan woke up with his face tickled by the early sun rays, dancing on and off his face to the rhythm of the tree branches swaying in the wind.

This is it. He felt a shudder in the pit of his stomach. He still couldn't figure out the reasons for his ordeal, as hard as he tried to make sense of it all. He thought of his father and remembered wondering why he'd seemed more distant and preoccupied in the last few months. *Does this have something to do with him rather than me? Maybe somebody is after him and somehow I got dragged into this, like David said.*

Realizing that he was going in circles again, he decided to get up, thank his hosts, and leave for his rendezvous with David.

Jules offered to walk with him back to the city and he gladly accepted. Going through the forest was not the easiest thing to do, and besides, he wanted to see if he could convince her to stop being so angry with him.

"How long have you been with the Scrappies?" he asked.

"About three months. Do you remember the last snow in March? That night, Tom found me in the forest and took me to the house."

"What were you doing in the forest?"

"Running away from home."

"Why?" Allan asked before thinking.

"Didn't like the rules," Jules answered casually.

"The rules?" he felt very confused. "What rules?"

"Stop prying. I just needed a change of air, all right?"

"I'm not prying. I just want to get to know you better. I've never met anyone like you." He could feel her reluctance to talk about herself, but didn't know how to make her confide in him.

"Lucky you. Less headaches and sarcasm that way."

"Without you I'd be dead now." Allan wished she'd make this a little easier on him. He changed the course of the conversation, since that seemed to be what was making her snappy. "Okay. Forget talking about yourself if you don't want to. How many Scrappies are living in the compound?"

"I don't know. A few hundred maybe."

"Don't they kill each other? Don't they steal from each other? It seems like a dangerous place to live."

"They do kill and steal, but those who kill get killed in return. Most of the Scrappies belong to one gang or another, forming something that resembles a family. That way they can live together and protect each other."

"I've heard of Scrappies who were caught stealing or causing some mischief in the city. They're taken to the Happy Endings clinic."

"Those were isolated cases. Some are mentally ill and they join the Scrappies, only to go back and roam throughout the city after a while. Others need supplies to survive and they venture into the city to procure them. Those who are caught never return. But the vast majority are people who couldn't live in the city any longer, like Mel or Daniel, or even me. We want one thing only, to be able to live a life of our choosing. We don't want to cause any trouble. Yet I'm afraid that one day they'll find out about my real status, all while working a job inside the system. I'd most certainly be taken to the clinic for that. I don't even understand why they call it Happy Endings. There's nothing *happy* about that."

"My father told me once that it started with the funeral being replaced with the celebration of one's life. In our society, people choose to end their life when they are too ill or simply tired of living, and thus the funeral home became a humane end to suffering, a place of happy ending."

"Still a screwed up name if you ask me. I'd never choose to end my life. Though I wish I were able to run far enough away to have a chance at a new beginning."

"That's why you hate the system."

"It's not really hate; it's anger, a feeling of being trapped. Not even being an Elite would make me happy. The whole society makes me sick. How did we end up this way?"

"It's because of the fog, I think. Everything is so small, I almost feel like I'm suffocating sometimes, except that I have a lot of virtual games that enlarged my world. If I can't escape the fog, I can always escape in a virtual reality of my choosing, climbing a mountain, or escaping to exotic beaches."

"Yet it's just a make-believe." Her tone was so sad, it made Allan want to reach out to her and comfort of her.

"Hey, would you like me to bring you to my home after this gets straightened out? I live in a truly kick ass mansion," he found himself saying, almost without thinking.

"I'm sure it is. I can't *wait* to visit an Elite home and see if it's just like in the reality shows," Her face lit up in mock excitement. "I just *love* watching Elites as they take a crap, brush their teeth, and eat their decadent meals. I can't believe people are really watching that. Let's make sure you don't die, then we'll see what can be done about changing the fate of the city and the opinion of Jules, all right?"

"Not sure if you're sarcastic or just bitter. Anyway, it's an open invitation, if everything goes well."

"Thank you. Well, we're here. David is probably already waiting for you in the street. Good luck!" With that, Jules turned around without waiting for him to reply and went back into the forest towards the Scrappie compound.

Allan looked back for a while to see her one last time, his heart heavy with concern for her, then walked to the scooter parked in the street, not far from where he'd come out of the forest. He nodded to David and then climbed into the scooter behind him.

"Where are we going?" asked David, turning his head slightly.

"Just take me to the Southeast Elite gate on the other side of the canal. I know the guards there and I have an excuse for why they don't have me on record for leaving the compound; unless the clone just did that, in which case, I have to think fast."

Without another word, David started off towards the city. As they approached the gate, he stopped the scooter and let Allan climb out. "Listen, in an hour I'll be here again, just behind the corner there so I'm not in plain view. I'll pretend something is wrong with my scooter in case somebody asks. Can't stay long, so come back if you can to let me know what happened. Depending on that, I'll either take you back or you'll go home. Are we good?"

"Yes, thanks for everything. One way or another we'll be in touch." Allan started towards the gate. He was relieved to see who was on duty.

"Hello, Fletcher. Having a good day so far?" Allan asked. Fletcher was a tall and very fit youth, sitting on a bench a few feet away from the guard cabin in the shade of a tree, reading a magazine.

"Master Allan, everything all right with you, sir? I don't think I have you on record for leaving home today," Fletcher said, while getting up from the bench. He took a tablet from his pocket and began scrolling through the data.

"I'm fine, of course. I was in a friend's car. Didn't want people to know I was sneaking out. Wanted to have some fun on a Friday night, you know? Behind the gate is nothing if not boring, if you know what I mean."

"Sure, but still, we should know. What if something were to happen to you?"

"Something did happen to me. I got laid, ha! You should have seen her big tits, middle of a wasp and a firm, round ass," Allan explained the details of his supposed adventure with his hands forming the contour of a woman's body.

The guard had no chance to doubt that everything was true, as his face got redder and his eyes and ears tried to absorb every word as if his life depended on it.

That was easy, Allan thought as he made his way home. Not long ago he'd been one of those boys, his life solely about games and girls, but now it seemed a lifetime ago.

8

At the southern border of the city, Tom was struggling to put one foot in front of the other, walking in the deep fog.

"I can't move a step further. Please, please let's go back!" In the milky air, Tom could hear his friend's voice, sounding as if the man was in great anguish. "Tom, please brother, my heart is racing. I think I'm on the verge of a heart attack." A thump followed. The man had dropped to the ground.

"Serge, get up. Get up, man, just one more yard. That's all I'm asking."

"I can't. Honestly, that's it for me. I've reached my limit."

"Okay, then get up and let's go back. We did better than last time. By twenty yards, I'd say. We did well." The two silhouettes started back, supporting each other at the waist.

In the bright light of Saturday morning, the two friends collapsed against a fence, right outside an Elite property, with their backs to a beautiful mansion a distance away. Facing the dense wall of fog, seemingly impossible to penetrate, they were trying to make sense of their latest adventure.

It had always been hard to walk in the fog. It was never that bad when they first started, but the deeper they went, the worse it got, until they hit some kind of psychological wall of panic. It happened without exception each time they had tried it.

"This time it was like I was walking into the midst of some vicious creatures that would start nibbling at my flesh at any moment. Then I started itching and it was like there were a thousand ants all over me. My heart was racing and I felt like it was going to burst. What did you feel?" Serge asked.

"More or less the same thing," Tom answered. "But we both know it's always been like that. It's been bothering me ever since we tried it the first time. We always carry the instruments with us, but there's nothing there. No ants in our pants, so to speak. So why are we so scared? Why the panic?"

"I don't know, but I beg you, no more tonight. My nerves are shot." He started to pull at his short hair, his head between his knees. Tom could see his hands were shaking.

"There must be *something* beyond the fog. And why doesn't it lift, ever?"

The whole city was surrounded by it. Tom had tried in other places. Other people had tried as well. Nobody could conquer the panic attack that followed. Serge turned to Tom, "Have you ever tried it through the old downtown? I've never been there. It's too scary with all the freaky Scrappies wandering around."

"Don't talk like that about them. You know very well I'm one of them now. But, yes, to answer your question. It's pretty much the same. On the other side of the skyscrapers there's the lake. Once I took out an old boat and when I reached the fog, I looked back. I got a better view of the whole area. This beastly fog surrounds the whole city in a large circle."

"What if the whole world is in the fog? What if we're the only ones alive?"

"Come on now. That's the kind of garbage they teach in schools, in history class." He imitated a booming voice, "*Lost forever is the Earth we knew before the time of the quakes. We're on our own, saved from the cataclysm, fortunate survivors in our beautiful little world.* Do you really believe that?"

"Can you prove that it's a lie? We haven't seen anything else, no matter how hard we tried. How long have we been doing this and how far have we gone? A hundred yards here, two hundred there, and what? Nothing!"

"Then we have to start thinking outside of the box. For example, if the limit to our expedition is largely imposed by our fear factor, let's eliminate that from the experiment."

"How will we do that?"

"We'll use the auto-platform. I lay down on it, you tie me to it and knock me out with the brainwave modulator. Then, you remotely drive the platform into the fog for as long as the remote works, while watching on the camera. You wake me up remotely. If I see nothing but fog and I can't bear the panic, I'll knock myself out, but not before I communicate with you to start driving me back. If I feel no panic, I'll venture to walk farther on foot. That might just do it." Tom felt pretty excited as he was talking.

"Look here," Serge countered. "Why not send the auto-platform on its own? Equipped with a camera and all the sensors, it could penetrate anything you would. It will record everything, without the need to jeopardize your life."

"Tried it already. I sent the platform by itself. It reached the distance limit for the capabilities of the remote control unit and it recorded nothing but fog. I hope to get farther on foot."

"All right, you've convinced me. Let me know when you want to meet and do it. I have to get all the stuff ready. How many platforms, how many modulators?"

"Two or three of each would be best. Maybe we convince a couple of our trusted comrades to come as well. It makes sense to send more than just one man. I'll let you know of anything else I might need." Tom was ready to leave, but Serge seemed to have something on his mind. "Is there anything else you'd like to say?"

"Tom, how long have you been in hiding? Almost four months. Isn't it time for you to come back?" Serge's voice showed how troubled his old friend was.

"Come back to what, Serge? Have we found out who wanted me dead? Do you have a lead on the conspirators?"

"Not yet, but how much longer can you stay in that place? I don't know what to do. Everything looks normal. I would just confront the city council, hold them accountable for what happened to you."

"And how do I do that? Do I go to them and tell them somebody wanted to kill me, so I staged my own death and a new *me* appeared out of thin air and took my place? Even if I manage to do that, somebody will have me killed later. Do you remember how it all began? I started to talk about the census. In fifty years we went from almost a million people to only a little over a hundred thousand. Maybe my math is a little rusty, but that's a pretty terrible growth rate for such an advanced civilization."

"The council told you that maybe it's nature's way of downsizing the population to a sustainable level, considering the small size of our world."

"Then I asked why we have negative growth when some people have clones to help prolong their lives."

"Only a small number of the population uses clones, though, the Elites. The technology is very expensive, which is why the Professionals use mostly cloned genetic material."

"Right, that's what they said too. I argued that maybe we should instead spend our credits on improving the lives of the Servers instead of spending so much on clones. That led me to the question of why there is an entire west wing of clones in the cloning facility for the leaders of our city. They're totally separated from the rest, heavily secured and costing us a small fortune for the upkeep."

"It's to ensure continuity of leadership and security in case of an uprising or a terrorist attack."

"Are you kidding me? What uprising? What terrorist attack? Our people are so dulled by all the Digiscreen shows and the video games, they take no interest in anything else. As for the outside world, nothing's happened in fifty years. Our security forces wouldn't even know how to fight an uprising or an attack, in spite of their ongoing training. Nobody has any real battle experience. We don't even need to fight the Scrappies, poor bunch of souls."

"Which brings me back to the fact that for over three months you haven't done anything to change your situation. And I don't know how to help. So you tell me what our next move is."

"I will, when I figure out what that is. Tell me, is my son all right?"

"He's a happy go lucky type of fellow. Games and girls, those are his top priorities."

"Good to know. I miss him a lot. Keep an eye on him for me. I promise to do my best and come up with a decision soon. And, Serge, brother, thanks. I'll send the messages via the usual channel. Stay alive!" Tom grabbed his backpack and took off.

9

Allan walked on the street leading to his house and passed a few joggers who acknowledged him with a short hand wave or a nod, all while keeping their eyes simultaneously on the street and the hyper-googles they were all wearing.

He arrived home without incident, but suddenly an odd feeling of insecurity enveloped him, as if his subconscious mind was sending him alarm messages. He decided not to go through the front entrance. Instead, he went through the back, circling around the great mansion he called home. On Saturdays and Sundays all the Servers had the day off and retired to their quarters nearby, once they ensured that food was cooked and ready to be warmed up and served.

The gardeners also kept a low profile. His father liked to enjoy some time on his own on the large lawn behind the house, where the tennis court and swimming pool were ready to be used.

Only the live-in maid was there, ready to do whatever was needed to keep her employers comfortable and well taken care of.

He approached the house from the back, walking stealthily and taking cover behind the trees and bushes that created archways above walkways covered in limestone and manicured to perfection.

The large patio doors leading to his father's office were open to let in the fresh, fragrantly scented air of roses and honeysuckle planted nearby. He could hear his father's voice speaking on the videophone, his familiar deep baritone voice emanating confidence and command.

He longed for their old times together, to once again feel protected and loved. And yet, he couldn't remember the last time his father had embraced him. It was surely many months ago, as if his father had decided it was time to wean him out.

He had almost stepped inside when he heard parts of the conversation, "Yes, it's been taken care of… in the incinerator, of course… yes, it's confirmed… the boy does not even know he's a clone… soon... it's going to look like an unfortunate accident… don't worry, I'll take care of it…. I had to, he knew too much… the other one will die as we planned initially… all right then," and he hung up.

Nothing had affected Allan more in his entire life than that one conversation. He felt completely numb. His knees seemed to give up on him, then his body started to shake uncontrollably, as if the dead of winter had settled into his bones. *Who is this monster? My own father. What is going on?*

His mind was going in circles, one question leading to others even more frightening. What, and why and when had it started? Who was involved? How many of them were in on this terrible plot of assassination and was he the primary target or just a peon in a big war game of sorts?

From deep inside him came a will to live, a will so fierce it enveloped him like a tidal wave. He would prevail and he would see the end of this if it took him the rest of his life. Suddenly, he remembered his clone and the fact that he was also in danger of being killed at some appointed time in the future.

I don't even know what I'm not supposed to know.

He pondered briefly and then put the thought on hold to attend to more pressing business: saving his clone, and hopefully making an ally of him. *None of me will die.* In spite of the dire situation, he found that latest thought hilarious.

He turned around carefully and tried another back entrance to the house, one that took him to the kitchen. It was used by the Servers coming in and out during the week.

The door was closed, but rarely ever locked, so he opened it carefully and slipped inside. He took the Servers' staircase up to the second floor where his apartment was and opened the door to his study room.

As he stepped inside, he felt a blow to his head, and crumpled to the floor.

"My God, you're my clone," he heard a voice. "What are you doing here?"

He opened his eyes and looked at his mirrored image, "*You* are my clone."

"Are you okay?"

"Back off, man. What was that, a bat?"

"You bet it was. You entered my house. I thought you were a burglar."

"Listen closely." He sat up with a groan. "*I* am Allan, the original Allan. You're my clone and you took my place a day and a half ago." Noticing that his counterpart looked frightened and ready to scream for help, Allan took a step back, raised his arms above his head in a surrendering motion, and continued.

"Please, don't say anything until I'm finished. It's a matter of life and death, for both of us." He saw the clone looking as if he was ready to listen, and he continued. "Did something unusual happen to you last Thursday night?" Then he lowered his arms and sat on the floor.

The clone hesitated for a moment. "Actually, yes. After a hard training day, I went to the Imaginarium, then came home and went straight to bed. I woke up some time after midnight with a terrible headache and a feeling of not knowing where I was. I'd had a dream of floating in a tube and it felt so claustrophobic… I woke up in a sweat. Then I relaxed because I realized I was in my own bedroom."

"The tube," Allan explained, "was not a dream, it was an actual memory you had, because you were kept in a tube filled with amniotic fluid your whole life until Thursday night. This is when they took me to the hospital and replaced me with you."

"Who would do that?"

"That doesn't matter right now. Tell me, do you remember being at the hospital at all?"

"No, nothing."

"What about going to the Imaginarium?"

"I remember that vaguely, bits and pieces, I apparently won."

"It's odd you don't remember the details. I know exactly what my strategy was." Suddenly a thought came to him. "Wait a minute, the game! It must have been the trigger for the replacement. But why?"

"I think you're crazy," the clone replied. "I'm going to call Father."

"No, no, don't do that. Please don't. Something terrible is happening to us." Allan started to tell the clone the whole story of his misfortune, and then his rescue, his coming back home, and finally the discovery he made while listening to his father's phone conversation.

As the clone listened to Allan's story, he looked as though he was going through a transformation. His boyishness, the innocent air of somebody living a sheltered life, was replaced by a new hardness of his features. His eyes began to bear a determination of his whole being, his chin pushed out with a stubborn will to triumph.

"This is absolutely crazy. I can't possibly be a clone." He stared at Allan, as if waiting for a challenge or for the nightmare to end. When nothing happened, he went and took a seat on the desk chair. He placed his head between his knees, trying to get his bearings back. "I don't feel any different. Should I?"

"I don't know, man," Allan replied. "I personally haven't met any clone, not that I know of, anyway."

The clone looked at Allan with questioning eyes. "What's going to happen to me, now that you're back?"

"I don't know. I'm not here to harm you, I just wanted my life back. So here I am. But I have to ask, do you feel as if your memories are yours?"

"Of course they're mine!" He stopped, as if trying to remember something. "Although, now that you mention it, I do feel a bit detached from them, like they have no power over me. I don't know how to explain it. It's more like what has happened in my life are things I've read in a book or watched on the Digiscreen, nice stories, but I can't quite understand why they should mean something. I had that feeling this morning, remembering I was going to play tennis today and wondered why I don't feel any excitement about playing, knowing all the while that I used to like the game. You think it's because I'm new on the job?"

"Maybe. Tennis is a great game, but I can see your point. If you never truly experienced the thrill of the challenge and the physical exertion of your muscles while playing, probably your brain can't force excitement about it."

"You know what else, this morning I was thinking how I'd like to be called Lan, does anyone ever call you that?"

"No, I've never cared to be called Lan."

"Then that's the first thought I can claim for myself. Might as well use the name Lan, now that there are two of us..."

"Why didn't you call father the moment you laid eyes on me?" Allan asked. "I mean, when you hit me over the head. Why not rat me out right away?"

"I don't know. I was curious, and intrigued. But I didn't feel any revulsion, if that's what you mean. More like you were my twin brother or something like that. I'm sorry I hurt you."

"Then you're a better man than me, because to tell you the truth, the first thing on my mind after what happened was to find you and kill you and be back again, just like before."

"I can't possibly be better. I'm *you*, remember?" Lan gave him a mischievous look.

Now that the air was cleared between them, Lan asked Allan a lot more questions about what had happened and how he'd gotten out of the hospital.

Allan felt a slight fear at sharing so much with somebody he'd barely met, even though the latest developments required him to make allies very quickly. "Listen Lan," he said, "I trust you, but please keep quiet about everything I told you." They both froze suddenly at the sound of a voice downstairs.

"Father is calling," said Lan. "We planned to go out for lunch today."

"Then I'd better get out of here. Look, I can't even begin to imagine how hard it must be for you to accept what I'm telling you. Think about all we've discussed. You can't stay here for long. See if you can get a sense of anything out of Father at lunch."

Lan agreed. "How about I meet you tomorrow morning behind the Servers' compound? I'll see what I can find out and maybe then we can work together."

"You sound like me," Allan said, smiling. "I'll see you tomorrow." They shook hands and Lan surprised him with a sudden brief embrace before leaving the same way he'd come in.

10

"Who wants cookies?" Tom called out as he entered his Scrappie house later in the day. Jules and Mel came racing at him.

"Goodness gracious, girls, how old are you? Here, there's enough for all." He opened a tin can for them to take some.

"I just love the way you spoil us. Makes us feel like a real family," Mel exclaimed with cookie crumbs flying out of her mouth, her eyes dancing. The taste of the cookies left her suddenly homesick. Seeing Jules so intent on telling Tom everything that happened during his absence, including Allan's rescue, she went back to the kitchen to finish preparing supper and to hide from the others her unexpected distress.

Mel had left home two months before, on the eve of her seventeenth birthday, just as spring was in full swing, the promise of a new beginning giving her courage. She had met Jules while being admitted to the hospital. Jules wouldn't let her go back to her home and old life, not after what had happened to her.

She finished preparing supper and then went outside to sit under her favorite tree and gaze at the sunlight filtering through the leaves. *Mom, Dad, why did you do this to me? Why didn't you love me back? Was I not good enough? Why did you have me, then?* She knew her case was not that special. *How many more sad sons and daughters are out there like me?* She wished there was a way for her to help them.

Her story was a typical one. Her parents liked to take all of their frustrations out on her, in bursts of explosive rage. Then they hit her: the back of a hand from her mother, a foot in the stomach from her father. It never happened at the same time, just when one or the other was having a bad day and she dared to ask a question right in the middle of a most dramatic turn in the movie her mother was watching or walked in front of the Digiscreen when her father was playing with the controls.

Occasionally, they would apologize to her and yell at each other for being out of control in front of the child, but most times they just resumed their show or game or whatever else there was on, ignoring her silent, shaking sobs. She never dared to cry out loud, not after she'd been locked in a closet for a whole day.

Even though she sometimes felt that it was her fault, she often couldn't even figure out what she'd done wrong. She loved her parents and she wanted to make them proud of her, so they would love her back. She kept finding excuses for them; they were just going through bad patches in life and had no patience left for her.

She couldn't remember her life at home being any different. The beatings became more severe as she grew older. She was taller and cried less, therefore they "worked" harder on her while drinking and watching their shows.

At school, nobody ever asked her about her family life or the conditions she lived in. Why would they? She was attending online courses from home, just like all the other Servers. Since Servers lived all over the place, online school was the standard. And her avatar looked always the same in the virtual classroom, whether she had been beaten up or not.

Her only joy was in the e-books she got from the city library and the lessons she learned at school. One of the teachers once sent her a personal message, writing that she had a good chance of receiving a scholarship, a once in a lifetime opportunity meant only for exceptionally gifted Servers. Her parents did not even hear her when she told them the news. They just mumbled something and continued to watch their respective shows.

One day, after her mother had had a bad night, she woke up with sharp pain in her abdomen and she waited the whole day for her parents to come home from work. By the time they took her to the hospital, she was unconscious. They waited for the doctor to tell them what had happened to their beloved daughter. The doctor told them that she had internal injuries without external manifestations. He awkwardly asked if they were aware of any abuse and they denied it vehemently. "How can you ask such a question? My little angel," her mother said, sobbing.

Mel had heard the conversation and later she admitted to the doctor that she had been beaten up many times. He had seen many children with no whip marks or bruises who had in fact been abused for long periods of time. Too many children died that way.

She met Jules, who had managed to put in a few hours as a cleaning agent at the Servers' hospital, and they became friends instantly. Jules invited her to come and live with her and Tom outside of the city after she got better; and she did get better. It took quite some time, but the doctors and nurses were really nice to her and never once hit her.

Once Jules took her under her wing, she never looked back, for Jules had such a strong personality and was very brave. Mel secretly envied her but she also loved her very much. And Jules loved her back, two sisters by choice.

"May I join you?" Jules asked, as she came outside.

"Sure," Mel smiled and pointed to a spot nearby. "Have a seat here, on the blanket. What did Tom have to say about Allan?"

"Well, he was concerned that we let a stranger in our home, but seemed to understand that we did what we had to do to help somebody in need. He also seemed surprised that an Elite went through such an ordeal. I don't blame him. It's not a common occurrence." Jules finished talking and seemed lost in thought all of a sudden.

"You like him, don't you?" Mel couldn't help but smile.

"Sure I like him, Tom is like a father to me," Jules answered, with a smirk on her face.

"Stop kidding around," Mel playfully slapped her on the arm. She wasn't about to let Jules get away so easily. "I meant Allan. You have a crush on him."

"No, I don't," Jules seemed revolted at the idea. "He's a brat. A self-centered, spoiled Elite. What makes you think that?"

"The way you talk around him, teasing, and trying to annoy him with your sarcasm. Like he's getting to your nerves. But you know he's not. He's cute, and you like him, don't you?" Mel persisted.

"He's different than how I imagined an Elite would be. He treats everybody the same way. And he looks at life with optimism. I would have been crushed in his place, knowing that I was replaced, but he found strength in his heart and courage to go and face his enemy."

"There you go," Mel smiled. "It doesn't kill you to admit it."

"All right then. So what if I like him? He's still a brat. His only concern was how to get away from here as soon as he could. We're still very different people. There's no future for me," she added softly.

"How can you say that?" Mel asked, trying to reassure her friend. "You are young and strong. You saved me. There are a lot of people out there who need saving. There's your future, Jules, helping out and making a difference in our lives."

"If I didn't already think that way, I'd kill myself right now. Or, probably not. Maybe it'd be more worthwhile to die trying to take down the clone makers."

"That's the Jules I know. Strong and feisty." Mel moved closer to her friend to hug her.

"What about you?" Jules asked, when they finished their embrace.

"What about me?" Mel asked, feeling scared to reveal her feelings, knowing full well Jules was going to ask her about the young man who had been visiting her dreams since the first day she had laid eyes on him.

"You are falling for Daniel. I see how you get flustered around him."

"He's too old for me. But I admire him, he's so smart," Mel tried to hide the tremor in her voice. "He has a Ph.D. I haven't even got a high school diploma yet. You know how bad that makes me feel? I can hardly open my mouth in his presence."

"Yet you're like a sponge when he's around, absorbing his every word," Jules insisted.

Mel shrugged. "I used to want to be a teacher, to teach kids natural sciences, but it can never happen without education. You know, I almost got a scholarship for college a few months ago. Now, my life is on hold. At the very least I can learn from him." She changed the subject to stop the tears stinging her eyes. "What's going to happen to us, Jules?"

"We'll live one day at a time. We'll take pleasure in the little things in our life and in the presence of our new friends. Who knows what tomorrow brings? So, Miss Mel, what's next for our new vegetable garden?"

And the girls started to talk about the work involved in growing their own food to add to the supplies that Tom, David, and Jules were already bringing to the table.

11

+Allan saw David bent down over his scooter, looking at the fuel cell components of his engine.

"I need to go back to the Scrappies," Allan said, approaching from behind. David nodded and closed the lid over his engine compartment, climbing on the scooter without a word. His eyes looked searchingly to Allan, as if checking if everything was okay, but Allan shook his head, signaling him to wait before asking anything else.

They left the scooter behind at Tony's bar and headed towards the forest. Tony was an old friend of David's and would know what to do if anyone asked about it.

In the shade of the trees, walking slowly towards the Scrappies' compound, Allan gave David all the details of his encounter with his clone, who he was already calling either brother or Lan. David didn't seem fazed by it and listened to every word quietly.

When he mentioned the conversation he overheard and how his father was in the middle of the assassination attempt on his life and also on a future attempt on Lan's life, David really became interested. "This seems like a larger plot than I imagined. Something big is at stake here. We have to figure it out somehow. I'm sure Tom will provide very good insight. Let's hope he's at home by now," They continued quietly the rest of the way.

They arrived at the house and went to the back where they could hear people talking.

Allan was in front, eager to share the news with his new friends, who he was unspeakably happy to see, as if they were the only sane people in an insane world. But a voice he recognized stopped him dead in his steps. A fury engulfed him, almost taking his breath away and he jumped into the house, like a panther on its prey, plowing into the man standing with his back at him.

"You son of a bitch!" he screamed. "You almost had me killed, you monster!" He placed his arms around the man's throat with a clear intention of breaking his neck. The man let himself fall to his knees and propelled Allan forward, slamming him on his back. Then he stood up and looked at him, eyes wide open with surprise.

"Allan, my boy, what in the world are you doing here?" he gasped.

"What am I doing here? What are *you* doing here?" he replied, getting up, ready to attack again.

"Hold your horses, boy," his father replied in a commanding voice, standing tall and strong. He turned to the others. "Can anybody explain what's going on here?" Jules had her arm around Mel for protection, while Daniel comically stood with a hand on his chin. David just stood in the doorway in shock.

Daniel finally broke the silence, "I guess this is why I thought Allan looked a little like Tom."

"Jules, *Allan* is the young man you saved?" Tom asked.

"Yes, he's the one," Jules said, in a weak voice.

"You never said who he was."

"I was getting there."

"Rather slowly. No matter now. Allan, I'm your real father. The man you've been living with at the house is a clone."

"That's a bit obvious at this point, don't you think? What the heck is going on here? How and when did you get replaced?" *I can't believe this is happening,* Allan thought.

"My name is Thomas Rusk, the head of Secure-IT," Tom explained for everyone else.

"What happened to you?" Allan was overwhelmed with curiosity.

"I got replaced with a clone almost four months ago. But, for the benefit of our young friends, please let me start from the beginning," Tom replied, looking at each of them in turn.

"It's about time I tell you what I know about what happened to our city, Elysian Fields, and the events that occurred over half a century ago.

"My grandfather was an inventor, a space pioneer, and a scientist at an old world space organization called NASA. He led the Deep Space Project and developed a technology that allowed mankind to truly reach for the stars. His vision was audacious and his dream was to die on Mars, not on impact, but as a colonist.

"In 2024, NASA sent to Mars the first intelligent machines to terra-form the red planet, to create an environment where people could thrive and build a sustainable civilization.

"Twenty years later, the Great Quake happened. We don't know for sure whether it was a natural occurrence or man-induced, but a chain of terrible cataclysms followed, a series of aftershocks even greater than the original quake that hit. It supposedly started at the New Madrid fault, somewhere south of here.

"A lot of people died in those days, and there was very little help coming from the outside. It seemed everyone had to deal with their own crisis. A few days later, absolutely all types of communication with the outside world ceased, as if we were truly the only people left on the face of the Earth.

"After that, fog surrounded the city in a large circle. It was such a thick layer that it was hard to see much, even if you went only a few feet inside it. The worst was that nobody managed to go through the fog deep enough to get to the other side. There seemed to be an energy field or some kind of psychological barrier, I really have no idea, but there was something that people couldn't overcome. It triggered a feeling of panic so overwhelming, it drove people back into the city. This happened a few years before my birth.

"What I saw as a young boy was a city being built on the outskirts of an older one, which had been mostly destroyed by the earthquake, and separated from the former by an accelerated growth forest.

"Since then we have been totally isolated from the outside world, if such a world even exists anymore. Sadly enough, we don't care much anymore about the history of mankind before the quakes, though we have archives full of data. Almost everybody lost interest in the past. You all know how we are encouraged to enjoy the present and our beautiful world, our city, and to escape in the virtual reality we have available at our discretion."

At this point, David intervened. "I always wondered why we didn't try harder to explore what is beyond the fog."

"Or why we stay glued to the Digiscreens," Mel added.

"We have little curiosity left at all. Nothing but complacency and passive aggression, escapism and overeating," completed Daniel.

"You're right," Tom agreed. "I was troubled by the same things. And I wanted answers to my questions, even as a young man. The hypernet shows, the video games, the virtual reality realm; they never interested me much. I used to get headaches from watching too much Digiscreen, so I preferred reading old books, which are incredibly hard to find. They made me realize that we live in what has become a decadent society."

"Have you tried to leave the city?" Jules asked.

"I attempted to leave the city a few times and go beyond it through the fog," Tom answered, "but I never managed to do so. I even tried remotely controlled model airplanes and hot air balloons, in the hope I could see through the cameras what was going on. But I only managed to lose them in the fog. There's something out there blocking us; either someone or something outside wants us kept in, or someone or something on the inside doesn't want us out. Another possibility is that there's nothing left out there on the whole planet, though I cannot accept that. Anyway, this leaves us with no solution but to stay put, as it were."

"How did you become the head of Secure-IT?" David asked.

"Since my family was one of the richest and certainly one of the most influential in the city, when I became of age, I took the helms of the family's company, Secure-IT. It had been established before the quakes as an information technology company.

"After the isolation, my father was put in charge of the city security, and he redefined the scope of his company with the mission to keep the people protected from eventual attackers from the outside. Then it evolved into ensuring that order within the city was maintained."

"Has society changed a lot since you took over?" Allan asked.

"The difference between the classes increased, especially once the Servers lost the manufacturing jobs that had provided them with a reasonably good income. In the last few decades, the factories in the city became fully automated and needed only a handful of Professionals to function."

"Nevertheless, people are satisfied; they have food, a roof above their head, and entertainment." David remarked.

Tom replied, "You are right, yet in the last few years, things have gotten worse. Our citizens seem to be more lost than ever, more withdrawn; like sleepwalkers, especially in the Servers' compound. Nothing interests them anymore, only food and entertainment. They go to work, then come home and just stay enraptured in front of the Digiscreen."

He continued, thoughtfully, "It was my job to watch the people, so it seemed like a downward trend, a dangerous one, as if our men and women had lost the joy of living altogether. Cases of tortured or neglected kids, beatings or total isolation, people applying to go to the Happy Endings Clinic to put an end to their life--those were scary incidents that soon became commonplace.

"I correlated that with the fact that some of our most prominent business owners and pillars of society seemed to change their behavior in subtle ways, making decisions that contradicted the moral values they used to hold dear. We found out that some of them were clones themselves, yet there was no record of what triggered the replacement or when it had taken place. However, we had to respect the governing rules of our society, which allows such transactions to take place confidentially.

"At about that time, I started to have doubts about the morality of even owning clones and thought of releasing Allan's double. I had never had one myself, just cloned genetic material.

"Then one day, at the end of February, one of my trusted associates, Serge, took me aside and told me plainly that an assassination attempt on my life was in progress. He had intercepted an encrypted message on the hypernet but couldn't determine its exact source or destination. Without further ado, we got into a car together with some explosives, cloned organs, and blood that belonged to me, and he drove me away from the office.

"Somewhere along the road, we got out of the car and he remotely started it again and slammed it into a tree. The car burst into flames. I went into hiding, and we waited for the announcement of my presumed death, hoping we could identify the players. But no announcement was made. Instead, a new *me* was in charge of the company and living in my house, with no word of what had happened. I've lived with the Scrappies ever since, keeping my head down and trying to figure out a solution."

12

"Now things are starting to make sense to me," Allan began. "I had a gut feeling something was going on with you, Father. For the past few months, you seemed more distant and preoccupied. I just thought that it was me growing up and changing, but in fact it was you who had changed. And then there were some small details and stuff we had done together that you didn't seem to remember. How could I be so stupid and not realize it wasn't you?"

"Don't blame yourself, son. It was safer for you that way. Just imagine what would have happened had you started raising too many questions. I am so sorry for not being there for you!" Tom's voice almost broke in a sob. "Thank goodness you're all right!"

"Honestly, what I'm having the most trouble with is the fact that you basically abandoned me to live with a clone, one whose motives you had no idea about. What were you thinking?" Allan felt a deep hurt in his heart, even though he was somewhat ashamed that this was all playing out in front of his new friends.

"I was afraid, and I had no real plan," Tom pleaded for understanding. "I thought that you were safe, and I had some people watching over you, Serge included. I would have come out of hiding at the slightest sign of danger for you, you have to believe that."

"Let's leave it at that for now," Allan conceded. "I need to share with you what happened to me today, as it sounds like this is all tied together somehow." He told them the whole story, including about how exactly he found out that his presumed father, the clone, was the one who had planned his death.

"It said that I knew too much. Except that I don't know what it was referring to. Talking to Lan, I found out that he did not have the full memory of the Imaginarium or of the hospital, so I'm going to venture and say that the game I played with my friends triggered the other events."

"What game was that?" Tom asked.

"It's called the *War of Sovereign Nations*. I must have stumbled upon some kind of information it couldn't afford to get out, so they tried to have me killed."

"Are you sure nothing happened to your friends?"

"As a matter of fact, no, I don't know that. I'll have to find out from Lan. I'll get him to call on them."

"You'd better give us all the details of the game and perhaps together we can draw some ideas as to the real cause of the attempt on your life."

At this moment, Jules intervened. "Don't say anything until I come back! I forgot to close the chicken coop door and take the goats to the shed."

As she opened the back door, she slammed it onto someone's face. A tall person stood on the porch and Jules was able to make out Allan's face. "The clone!" she yelled. Her first instinct was to put her arms in front of her and kick him in the groin with one knee. "Help!" she screamed, while Lan fell to his knees.

Everybody was up with whatever they could grab for a weapon. Allan got outside first and, seeing Lan down, signaled the others to calm down, then helped him up and inside the house.

"Sorry, everyone," Lan exclaimed, taking a seat offered by Mel. "I didn't mean to scare you, I was just trying to find my brother." He let off a noisy sigh and lowered himself in a chair. He looked up at Allan. "I'm lucky I found you."

Allan looked at him suspiciously. "How did you get here? I thought we agreed to meet tomorrow."

"Before you left, I placed a tracking device on you. Remember the hug? I'm sorry, but I felt like if I needed to leave the house suddenly, I needed to know where to go. I took a cab to the Server compound. The hard part was crossing the forest on foot. Got scratched more than I care to remember. As soon as I was out of it, I used the tracking software on my tablet to pinpoint the device Allan was carrying, and it got me here pretty easily."

"Are we safe? Did anyone follow you?"

"No one followed me, I'm sure of it. I'm sorry, I just couldn't stand the fear of being killed anymore. I need as much help as you do. So I figured, why not get it from the same people you are? Oh, and hello, Father," he addressed Tom.

"Hello yourself. You don't seem confused to see me sitting here," remarked Tom casually, finally getting over the initial shock.

Lan shrugged. "I figured it out. No matter if I was a clone or an original, my real father would never have me killed. So he must be a clone too. And yet somebody must have re-programmed his mind or else why would he want us dead? Something bad is going on there. That's why I decided to leave. And here I am."

"Not a wise decision. He's going to look for you, and when he cannot find you, he'll employ all the resources he has to track you down. We'll be in extreme danger, because the first thing he'll do is raid the Scrappie compound. Have you thought of that?"

"Am I supposed to just sit there waiting until the hammer falls? Can't you keep me safe?"

"I believe you are safer living there. The clone, who I guess we can just call Thomas for now, can't pretend you got sick at home and died, not when we have excellent healthcare and enhanced immune systems. He'd probably get you involved in something a bit unusual, like rock climbing, or some other type of adventurous activity that would allow for an *accident* to happen."

"Besides, we needed you to keep an eye on him and tell us of his whereabouts, schedule, and report any unusual activity," Allan added.

"Easy for you to say. Why don't you take my place?"

"Because I don't know whether Thomas has a way of telling that I'm an original or not. You, on the other hand, don't have to fake it."

"Are you on our side for real? It seems weird how easily you got convinced to go against Thomas and join Allan's side," David intervened.

"I have nothing to hide. My life is in peril. Allan heard what Thomas said, that *the other one*, meaning me, will die soon, as planned. What can I possibly gain if I turn you in?"

"Lan's right. I heard it clearly enough. That's why I rushed to help him instead of trying to get rid of him, "Allan said, defending his brother.

"Thanks, I guess," Lan replied. "Getting rid of me, like in *murdering* me. I like this world of yours less and less. You kept me in stasis, just in case, like I was a disposable item. And here I thought I'd gained my freedom, when instead I was just brought to some sort of twisted existence, and now I'm fighting for my life. You guys are crazy."

"Our world is definitely a bit mad and out of control," Daniel jumped into the conversation. "But you have to understand, the original intention was not to create full clones. I guess we started doing it simply because we could. And once we started on that path, there was no limit to where it could take us, other than our own imaginations. When somebody with a twisted mind puts a spin on the whole affair, everything just goes crazy."

"That's how we ended up in this mess," said Jules. "Replacing humans with clones is inherently wrong. I've been a part of it at the hospital and it freaks me out every time, having to take the dead to the incinerator once someone else had their memory. How can people delude themselves into thinking that they're hugging their dear child or brother or mother when they're just holding a product of a lab? Sorry, Lan, I don't mean to upset you, but in all honesty, I believe that clones are an aberration. We should terminate all the experiments and only keep the technology for cloning body parts."

"Jules, I hope you don't truly mean *terminate*," Tom stepped in, with a look of great distress on his face. "I thought you knew, but obviously not. There's no real easy way to say it, but *you* are a clone."

Jules stared at Tom, incapable of comprehending what he'd just said.

"Have you lost your mind?"

Tom slowly got up from his chair and got close to Jules. Looking gently at her, he knelt in front of her and said, "You look so much like your mother, Jules. We went to school together, ages ago. She had a daughter who died. You are that daughter's clone, my darling."

"That's not possible, it must be a mistake," Jules pleaded with them, grasping desperately at Tom's arms.

Then she got up suddenly and ran out of the house through the front door. Mel started after her, but Tom put his hand on her shoulder and stopped her. "Let her be. She needs to figure things out for herself."

He turned to the others. "It's getting late and we had a lot happen today. I suggest we reconvene tomorrow with a clear mind. You can spend the night here, Lan. You can always explain it away with a night out with friends, something Allan did many times." Both Tom and his sons smiled at this point. "But tomorrow you have to go back home. I'll take you back to the Server compound; you can go further on your own. David, as always, you're welcome to stay over. Jules is going to come back to her senses and will be back in no time. I trust her good judgment. Good night everybody." He went upstairs, leaving the others to get ready for the night.

13

Jules ran as far as she could into the early night and stopped, gasping for breath, at the edge of the forest. *Why is this happening? Why me? I'm losing my mind. This cannot be. I can't deal with it. Oh God of heavens, am I real? Do I have a soul? Am I created? Did I just appear out of nowhere? I'm losing myself, like I never existed. But, how can that be? I have feelings, I like to help people, I have friends... Do I have friends still, now that they know about me? Oh, God, if you exist, please don't let me lose my mind. Tell me I'm a human being, not an animal or a lab experiment. Oh, no, mother, mother, what have you done to me? How could you do it, who are you?* Suddenly the thought struck her that her mother must know the answer and she desperately needed to know. Now.

She got up and ran in a frenzy through the dark forest, scratching her arms, falling a few times, stumbling through the dark and, when she couldn't run anymore, she walked until she arrived at her mother's doorstep. How she had wanted to forget those days of her former life. Yet, she had still yearned for her mother's embrace, like when it was just the two of them.

Her stepfather had moved in when she was about twelve. For four long years she'd had to endure the "attention," the smooth talk. *Let's be friends. Be good to me and we'll have lots of fun together.* Her mom, happy to share the burden of her Server life with a strong man, did not want to see it. She wanted someone who could love her just as she was, an ordinary woman and single mother.

Jules resisted his advances and made sure to never be alone with him. She would rather be in the streets walking until the time of her mother's return, just in case he happened to come home early. She used to watch by the window to see him approaching the building, and when she spotted him she would run to the fire escape ladder and go down to the street or up to the roof to gaze at the early stars.

The roof was where she met Bruce, her neighbor, looking at stars through an old telescope. Bruce understood what was going on without many words between them, and they spent many evenings together as he taught Jules all kinds of things about the heavenly realm.

When she turned sixteen, almost three months ago, her stepfather told her that she was old enough to feel like a woman. He said that he would help her feel that way. Somehow, one day he arrived home before she had a chance to escape and he came to her room, red in the face, glassy eyed, and started pulling her towards him.

Instinctively, she did what Bruce once showed her to do in self-defense and kneed him in the groin. The brute, who had not expected it from his "sweet girl," crouched in pain. In a moment, she was gone. She had no coat on her, feet with only socks on, running like a deer from a voracious wolf.

Tom found her in the forest hours later that night, half frozen and incoherent. He put his coat on her and carried her in his arms to his house on the other side of the forest. For a few days she could not remember who she was. Then, memories of people and things that had happened in her life came to her slowly. She never told them to anyone, including Tom.

After a couple of weeks, she left Tom's house for the first time and ventured back into the city, where she ran into Bruce. He introduced her at the hospital as his niece who needed a job. He took her ID card from her mother and told her that Jules was okay, but would not be coming home for a while.

And now, after all that time, Jules stood at the door, her heart pounding, not sure whether she could move on with this. Before she had time to decide, her mother opened the door with a garbage bag in one hand.

"Jules!" she exclaimed, the other hand reaching her mouth. "My God, you're home!" She dropped the bag to embrace her.

She backed away apprehensively. "Is he here?"

"No. No, he's gone. He left me." She moved aside as Jules hastily pushed her way in, without paying attention to the extended arms.

"Tell me who I really am," Jules demanded, without any preamble.

"What… what do you know?" her mother stammered.

"Just answer my question."

The steel in her daughter's eyes threw a shudder down her spine, and the middle-aged woman sat on the shoddy couch with a distant look in her eyes as she began her story.

She began by admitting she wasn't her mother. She'd actually been her live-in nanny, working for an Elite socialite. The original Julia had never been healthy. She had a bad heart, a birth defect that the lady of the house, her mother, did not want to acknowledge. She insisted all the tests had showed a perfect baby and that Julia was simply a true lady, fragile but not in need of a heart transplant. And yet she knew it in her heart not to be true, and she decided to order a clone.

It took several years for the clone to develop into a beautiful girl, even though the artificial growth rate had been highly enhanced.

The day came when the mother signed the papers to have her daughter put to death, and the clone sent to the house, all memories transferred from one to the other. The new girl was full of life, but she never went to her mother for affection or attention. When she scraped her knee or wanted to show off, she always went to her nanny.

Eventually, the lady felt as if she had a stranger in the house, not her beautiful pet girl. The original Julia had always been there, quiet and smiling timidly, pleased to be hugged between her mother's appointments.

Regret ate at her heart that she'd put her sweet, gentle little girl to death in order to get this boisterous, dirty tyrant, who was turning her immaculate house into a circus.

One day, the lady came to the nanny and discussed with her the options. Together, they decided it was better to send the clone away with her nanny under the guise of a tragic accident. After all, she was the living image of Julia and she deserved a chance to live. But the lady simply could not have her there in her presence any longer. She paid the nanny a handsome fee for her silence, lest bad fortune follow them both.

To the rest of the city, Julia perished in a terrible accident while her clone, becoming Jules, came to live with her new mother in the Servers' compound, far away from the Elites that would recognize her.

"How could you do that to me? Not telling me anything all these years?" Jules asked, her tears flowing openly down her cheeks.

"What could I say? You were so little when we left, not even five. It was for your own good, my darling."

"You could have told me later on, when I was able to understand. You had no right to hide from me who I was."

"How would that have helped you? So you could track down your real mother and maybe get yourself killed? When we left, she told me never to come back. That was not an empty threat. We should be grateful we were allowed to live. Jules, I love you so much, I was just happy to have the chance to be with you and raise you. I sacrificed my life for you, can't you see?"

"I can see the lies you fed me. And I can remember how you brought in that horrible man, and how you ignored me, not wanting to see what was happening in our own home, his advances, and his dirty looks in my directions. How could you do that to me if you loved me?'

"I'm so sorry. I wanted so much to have a family. When he came into our lives, I was so happy. I just thought he cared about you, because he was nice to you."

"Oh, how naïve can you be, mother!" Jules sighed. "I've been trying to tell myself it's over now, and he's gone. Tell me the truth, weren't you repulsed by me, being a clone?"

"How could I be repulsed? You brought joy to my life. I felt sorry for Julia, a little sick child, but when you came to the house, you were so full of energy, so playful, you had a great imagination. You changed me. You made me laugh, you came to *me* for hugs, and we played together. You were like a daughter to me, from the moment I set my eyes on you."

"I don't know who I am anymore, mother. I feel lost. Every time I had to clean up after a human being was replaced by a clone at the hospital, I felt so angry seeing clones taking over one's life. It didn't seem right. I hated them. And look at me now. I'm one of them. What can I do with myself? How will I live with this?"

"Jules, you are a human being. Not a machine, not a manufactured product, not a toy or an object. You are as human as I am. Don't let your anger hide from you the fact that you are human. You came from an embryo that had its DNA replaced with someone else's, that's all."

"But that girl had to die in order for me to come to life. How can I live with the fact I took someone else's life?"

"You did no such thing. Besides, Julia was very sick, her mother waited too long to make a decision to have a heart transplant done. The poor little thing was very weak. It might have worked, the transplant, but the choice was not yours or mine. Think about it, you had a chance at life, and they granted you that chance. Enjoy it, my darling. You are alive and strong and smart."

"And I have no place to live, no escape door to a different world. My life is doomed, nothing is in sight to make it better."

"You have just as many chances as any of us. What's in store for me? Work and lonely years ahead, with just the idea that one day I might decide to go to the Happy Endings clinic, to put an end to my life, either sick or depressed."

"Don't talk like that. You're still young."

"You are even younger, darling. My hope is that you will have a better life."

"How can it be better?"

"You have a lot of energy and are very smart. Who's to say you can't make life for the Servers better, or that you can't help change the human replacement practices you hate so much? The future is yours."

"Mother, I love you so much."

"I love you, too. Will you stay here with me?"

"I can't right now. One day, maybe I will want to come back," Jules smiled.

"I'll live with that hope then."

"And don't even think about Happy Endings, all right?"

Mother and daughter ended their conversation in a tight embrace.

14

The next day at dawn, Lan and Tom were already on their way back to the city. Tom was very concerned that Thomas would find out Lan hadn't been out partying after all.

"Who knows whether he's got somebody on your tail? Have you thought of that?" he asked Lan in a somewhat angry voice. "These are dangerous times, boy. You have to be extremely careful from now on."

"Would you mind not calling me a boy?" Lan asked, feeling slightly annoyed at Tom's tone of voice. "I don't like it, and I suspect Allan resented it too. It's condescending."

Tom appeared taken aback. "Allan never mentioned that to me. I'm sorry if that made you feel uncomfortable. I'm so used to seeing him, and now you, as a young boy." He paused for a bit before continuing, "I have to tell you, seeing the two of you together is very confusing for me. I was going to say *when did you grow up so soon*, but then, I was addressing Allan, not you. And yet, you are my son, too. I guess I'll need a bit more time to find the proper way to talk to you in a way that's appropriate."

"I understand perfectly how you feel," Lan decided to open himself up to this man, his father. "In my mind I keep calling you Tom. I thought Thomas was my real father, but then it turns out you're my real father, and yet neither of you are my father, or maybe both of you are. It's really screwed up."

"You're right. A complete mess… And guess what? We have to make sense of it all very soon, because they'll find out about us sooner or later."

"Do you know that when I came to the house last night, I wasn't entirely sure I was a clone?" Lan felt the need to continue on the topic they had started. "Part of me still wanted to believe that this was a game of sorts. I mean, everything Allan had told me made perfect sense, and logically I was convinced. Emotionally, I was a wreck. I felt totally lost and alone, scared and nervous that I would die any minute. Do all clones go through the same agony like I am?"

"No, not as far as I know," Tom replied. "According to my knowledge, the clones don't even know what they are. Imagine how *you* felt the day after you'd been brought home to live with Thomas, the thought never entered your mind until Allan told you otherwise, right? I believe that is the standard. I'm not saying that the family members haven't noticed some minor changes in temperament, or that there was no adjustment period, but I haven't heard of any major problems with clones slipping right into life as if nothing happened. For all intended purposes, they were the originals brought back to life."

The two stayed silent for a time. "That's very troubling to me," Lan said eventually. "How come the members of their families haven't realized they were dealing with different human beings altogether? How come *you* never suspected anything in your position of power? You could have said something, done something."

"But I didn't know for sure, Lan. I'm looking in retrospect now. I don't remember any instance when an original and a clone lived their lives in parallel. Even now, I can't tell whether you're just Allan continuing on a different path, as if you'd lived in a parallel universe."

"That's absurd! I'm not Allan, can't you see? I am a human being who had been dreaming desperate dreams in a tube filled with fluid, waiting to be awakened. An enslaved human being, not even knowing it… I can't even begin to imagine myself in suspended animation, waiting for the tube to rise so I could escape." Lan actually started to cry, angry over the thought of his prison.

"Lan, it's over now. You are free, my son. It's over." Tom's unsteady voice, as if fighting back his own tears, brought Lan back to the present.

"You're right, it's over. But my whole life has been altered by the knowledge of who I am. Nobody could ever understand me, except maybe Jules. She must be devastated. I'd like to believe that she'll be all right. I should have stayed, to wait for her to come back."

"Out of the question, Lan. You need to go back now. We'll see each other soon enough. And I'll let you know about Jules' situation. She's very strong, an admirable girl. And you two appear to have more in common than any of us thought."

"You may be right. If she can make it, so can I."

On that note, they got close to the edge of the forest, behind the Server compound, and Lan said goodbye to his father. With his mind still in turmoil, he decided to call him Tom from then on, not yet comfortable calling him father.

15

Sunday morning was bright and cloudless. Allan woke up feeling rested and at peace for the first time in days. He went downstairs to find David and Daniel eating in the kitchen, while Mel's voice could be heard outside feeding the chickens their breakfast.

"Scrambled eggs again?" he asked.

"There's a good supply of those from our feathery friends outside," David mumbled, with his mouth full. "Help yourself." He pointed towards the stovetop, where a pan was still half full.

"Where are Lan and my father?"

"Tom went to help Lan through the forest," Daniel replied. "He'll be back soon."

Sure enough, a short while after that, Tom came in and joined them at the table. "So, Allan, can I ask you more about the Imaginarium?"

"We should probably wait for Mel to join us," Daniel intervened. "She'd be upset if we started without her." He went outside to help Mel finish her work.

They moved to the living room to have more space, and Allan started to recollect his actions from a few days before. He told them about the sequence of events in the *War of Sovereign Nations* game. He talked about Brad and his traditional warfare approach. Then he moved onto Brent's cyber-attacks and nuclear war scenario.

Allan explained his own strategy and how the food had been laced with addictive chemicals, dulling people's minds, and he mentioned the great entertainment that would distract the people whose country he was planning to conquer.

"Thus, when my troops landed, nobody cared about what was happening to their country. They had lost any desire to fight, freedom becoming an empty word. I won without a shot being fired. In a way, it was less satisfying because there was no real war, as if I had been cheated of a fair victory," Allan concluded his story.

The others had been listening carefully, absorbing every word. After the story ended, everybody was quiet for a while, as if they were still under the influence of the emotions they felt as the story unfolded.

"Very interesting," Tom started. "The scenario you played brought about the similar results I've seen in the city. You remember me talking about our citizens, especially the Servers, losing interest in life, their whole existence centered on entertainment and food? I think you've just opened up the possibility that what's happening to our city is real, not just a figment of our imagination. I see no other reason for the attempt on your life."

But Tom was no closer to finding out the masterminds of the plot than before learning about the game. Even with his security contacts, he couldn't come up with any logical culprits.

"You may not have an answer, but think about it," Daniel intervened. "Allan performed an experiment, with the hypothesis being that a whole population can be manipulated into doing something without them realizing it. Thomas was probably afraid that he'd start thinking that way in real life, or that with some prior knowledge, he'd start noticing things in the city."

"That's true, since Lan seemed to have all my memories but those about the game. But how would Thomas know what I was playing?"

"Perhaps he has a way of connecting to the game," David speculated. "Who knows, maybe all the games we play are monitored and analyzed."

"The fact that the authorities don't do anything about the Scrappie compound, and that they don't care to keep us contained, shows that they are not concerned about an uprising or other dangers. Maybe it's because they already know everything," offered Mel.

"You're right," Tom added, "while to you it may seem that city security is simply lax, it's a proven fact that it's easier to control people that do not feel cornered. We have to leave them a way out. Otherwise, they become dangerous and lash out. We kept the Scrappies under control by ensuring that they have a choice of coming back to resume their existence in the former positions, after the initial rebellious stage was over. Meanwhile, the ones with real mental issues or leadership qualities, the potentially dangerous ones, we took them to the Happy Endings clinic."

"So what do we do?" Allan felt at a loss.

"I'd like to propose something." Daniel stopped briefly, deep in thought. "If I could conduct a field test, on a small population of mice, for example, perhaps we could draw some conclusions regarding the food. No offense, Allan, but I'd hate to just jump right to the conclusion that our food is contaminated. Yet based on the symptoms Tom mentioned before, and my observations, it is a definite possibility."

David was quick to jump on his idea. "In the meantime, I could dig up some background information about entertainment. I remember some friends talking about subtle messaging being layered into advertising during the last century. It seemed farfetched at the time and I didn't pay much attention. Maybe it could shed some more light on the situation."

"Very well," Tom concluded. "Let's do that, and then we'll regroup and see what we're up against."

They finished their discussion and David went back to the city to get some lab mice for Daniel to start his experiment. Tom went out too, to discuss with Serge the latest developments, and ask if there was anything his old friend could do to help, in addition to what they had already agreed upon.

Allan, Mel, and Daniel were left alone to speculate on everything that had happened.

A few hours later, in the middle of the afternoon, they were sitting outside on the back porch.

Jules and Lan turned the corner at the back of the house. Allan saw them coming and was unsure what to do, torn between anger of seeing his brother disobeying father's instructions and happiness that Jules was back and seemed all right.

"What are you doing here, man? I thought father told you not to come here except in an emergency," Allan started.

"I thought you'd like to know that Brent and Brad are all right. No harm came to them like with you, though it's hard to say for sure that no one got to them." Lan sat down on the porch. "And I wanted to make sure that Jules was all right. Don't worry," he added, seeing Allan's stare, "I'll go back before dark."

"It's true. I am a clone," Jules stated simply, taking a seat on a wicker chair. She told them everything.

"So do you feel any less of a human being, now that you know what you are?" Lan asked her, with no hint of sarcasm.

"It's weird to know that I'm the result of laboratory work. But then, am I me or just a collection of a poor girl's memories and a shadow of her soul? I don't even remember being sick or weak or anything like that, and apparently Julia was always sick. I have a hard time understanding this. Yet what I am has no bearing on *who* I am, Jules."

"I think," Mel ventured shyly at first, "that all human beings, whether originals or clones, have divine origin. I read a lot and it got me thinking that never once were we able to create a living cell from nothing. Manipulate yes, but not create. Even when we take the DNA and replace it with another person's, we're just playing God, nothing more. So my theory is that the essence of life, the soul, is something given to us and is unique, ours forever and ever. Our memories, our thoughts, they're external additions. You understand what I'm trying to say?"

"I think I do and I'd like to believe you," said Lan. "That way I can be at peace with the fact that it's still me when I have memories of things I've never experienced, some of them quite gross, I might add," he made a puking face looking at Allan, who smiled.

"Why does it have to be a god who has created life, etcetera, etcetera," intervened Daniel, his face quite intrigued. "It could just be that we were born, we live, and we die, end of story. Life could have come from outer space, other planets, you know, via meteors or comets, or simply through evolution."

"Ultimately, it's our choice to believe whatever makes sense to us," Mel continued. "I think that a soul such as mine, experiencing so much beauty and sorrow and pain and love cannot simply cease to exist at the moment of death. And if this is true, then I must have been created by something or someone immortal as well, probably in his image, because it was the best model to copy." She smiled shyly, as if apologizing for speaking so much, something that was unusual for her.

"You should know by now that the creation theory does not hold water," Daniel insisted. "It's no more real than the boogeyman. Every decent scientist will tell you that there's ample proof that evolution has been going on for millions of years. The human soul is just wishful thinking. We are extraordinarily ordinary, if you'll pardon my expression, there's nothing special about any of us. We will die and the energy field around our brain will disappear, our thoughts will vanish and we will immerse in a great ocean of nothingness."

"Stop speaking to me like I'm a child," countered Mel, her face becoming flushed. "First of all, I call it intelligent design, as well as creation theory, and it obviously implies an intelligent designer. You mock my faith, but what is your conviction if not faith? Your belief that things eventually change if given enough time over the course of billions of years, isn't that just another kind of faith? The universal law of entropy implies destruction, not creation. Everything in nature mutates, doesn't evolve, in my opinion. Tell me, if I drop a box with toothpicks on the floor, how many times do you think I would need to drop it before the toothpicks form your name, Daniel? Is a billion times enough? Or if I have all the components of a mechanical watch in a box, how many times should I shake it before it turns into a watch?"

Daniel just stood there, taken aback, Mel's passion seeming to make a very strong impression on him.

"I wasn't mocking you, and I'm sorry I upset you. It was just pure scientific debate."

"No, it was not just that. When we stop seeing the magic in the world, we are truly doomed, no better than a machine. That saddens me more than I can say." She went inside, leaving them all without a chance to reply.

"You didn't need to be so mean," Jules remarked. "She's a sensitive girl."

"I noticed that," Daniel muttered. "I care about her. We were just talking. It wasn't a personal attack."

"But she took it very personally," Jules continued. "And so do I. We're not just talking about abstract things, we're talking about how we feel about the world. We are trying to make sense of our existence. Without a moral compass, how do we know right from wrong? And who gives us the moral compass? Human beings change their opinions all the time. What was totally unacceptable a few decades ago has become the norm nowadays. Look what we've done with the clones. Maybe we need an absolute truth to guide us through life and only God can give us an absolute compass."

"Here we go again," Daniel lamented. "Sorry, but this is how I feel."

"I don't know about you guys," Allan said, attempting to change the subject, "but since clones are human beings, as proven to us without a doubt, don't you think it's a great injustice done to them? I mean, to harvest them for their organs? Who gave us the right to choose who lives and who dies?"

"That's why I told you I couldn't do it anymore," Daniel raised his voice appealingly. "We had the technology to grow organ tissue; whole organs, without the need of a whole human being. When and why did we start to harvest our own kind?"

"We should fight for the clones' freedom!" Jules volunteered with great excitement.

"Why not, let's do it!" Allan found himself joining in her frenzy.

"Do you really mean that? Are you willing to sacrifice your life to fight for this cause?" Lan seemed skeptical.

"Why not?" Allan felt his belief getting stronger. "Lan, the fact that you and I met, it's the chance of a lifetime, and I'm sorry you went through such an ordeal in order for that to happen. But you are alive and well now. I think we should stop developing clones and free the ones already in stasis."

"We can make things right," Jules agreed, "We can have a purpose so that our lives are not in vain."

Allan felt the energy in the air at unbelievable high level. *I can do something exceptional with my life.* The realization struck him with intensity.

"We're just a bunch of young people with no real power," Daniel's voice brought them down to earth. "We have no weapons, no allies, just a lot of enthusiasm."

After a brief letdown, Allan felt his willpower resurface, his clear determination stronger than ever. "We have my father and his connections at Secure-IT. We're smart and we have each other. Together we can accomplish something great. And if we fail, so be it. Our lives will have had a meaning beyond ourselves."

"When did you get so enthusiastic about life?" Daniel asked. "Just yesterday you were trying to get your life back without much concern for anything else."

"A few days ago I was just a kid playing a game. Today I have a father and a brother to fight for. And new friends who need me. Isn't that enough?" said Allan defensively.

"It's more than that. You have guts and passion and a spirit of fairness. One day you'll be a great leader." Lan's words surprised Allan more than anything. *He knows me better than I do myself,* thought Allan. *It feels good to have a brother who believes in you.*

"Then there's nothing to worry about. We're in good hands," Daniel's bitter tone surprised Allan, but not for long, because he continued. "Sorry for the sarcasm. Why don't we wait and discuss this with Tom and David? For what it's worth, I'm in, and will do anything in my power to help."

"Are you sure about helping, Daniel? 'Cause you don't sound sure," Jules remarked.

"Sure I'm sure. I just thought we were getting way overboard with our expectations. I like to keep it real, and manageable, that's all."

16

A few days later, David came back to Tom's house in the Scrappie compound. He had a carrier from which Daniel recovered a large family of mice, ready to be used for an experiment on the food.

The two brothers went outside, and Daniel started to place the mice in two cages.

"One cage will hold the mice who will be fed city food. We'll call them city mice. The other one will hold the mice fed on grains and cheese. We'll call them the country mice. It will take me a few weeks to determine the effect of the food on the two groups, if any. It's the best I can do."

David looked at his brother. Daniel seemed glad to be engaged in something other than his books. *How much I'd like you to come back with me*, David thought, but he said nothing, because Daniel refused to talk about anything that involved him going back to the city.

"What are you reading these days?" David asked.

"The same stuff as before. All the books I found in an old house are science fiction ones. The owner must have been an avid sci-fi reader, but I think she or he was obsessed with dystopian societies."

"What's *dystopian*?" Mel asked, coming outside to join the brothers, with Jules and Allan following her.

"Dystopia is a bad society, a twisted world where people are oppressed and live in misery or in frightening conditions. Most of them don't even realize their lives are not as they should be. It was used in stories of the future, written by people who were concerned about the way things were going in the world."

"At the opposite end, there is Utopia, a place where everything is just perfect, in an ideal state. I don't think many people wanted to read about that. Where there's no conflict, there's no action, which makes for a poor plot for a book," David commented. "Why your fascination with such books, Daniel?"

"They got me thinking about our own society. Reading those books made me realize that we might live in such an altered world."

"The Elites would disagree with you," Jules intervened in a sad voice. "They live in Utopia."

"But they would be wrong," Daniel explained. "Neither the Elites nor anybody else living here without knowledge of what's going on could objectively consider our city a utopian or dystopian society. You see, it is hard to see the world with preconceived ideas when you are a part of the system. One has to go through a drastic transformation in order to do so, or get out of the system completely to better understand it."

"And this is what happened to all of us," Allan completed Daniel's idea. "We're able to see how bad things are when faced with adversity."

"That's right," Daniel smiled in Allan's direction. "I'm glad we think along the same lines. I think we live in one of the worst nightmares a mediocre science fiction writer could conceive."

"It could be worse. We could be tortured or something," Mel exclaimed. "And why do you say a *mediocre* writer?"

"Because there is no way out. A great writer would concoct a solution to this, an amazing way out, a bunch of heroes saving the world."

Allan approached and placed his hand on Daniel's shoulder. "Man, this is not a science-fiction book. It's for real. Let's find a way out by ourselves. Remember what we talked about last Sunday? There's hope, my friend."

"Speaking of which, is Tom home?" David inquired. "I have some information I'd like to share with you all."

"He's eating, just got home a short while ago," Mel replied. They went inside to discuss the latest developments.

"Regarding the entertainment connection," said David, when everybody was seated in the large living room. "What's been bothering me for the longest time is the ability of people to watch the Digiscreen endlessly, no matter what's on. Being a software engineer, I'm involved quite a bit in game development, and I also collaborate with graphic artists and commercial developers.

"As I promised you a few days ago, I talked to a couple of friends about the possible ways of influencing people's minds. I told them that I was just curious, in light of our previous conversation on the subject.

"They showed me some archived files on the matter, and we discussed at large the various ways the media manipulates our minds. The most powerful tool utilized was based on subliminal perception. It's been around for quite a while and what I've found is that in the past it's been used extensively in everything that involves communication of any kind."

"And what exactly is subliminal perception?" asked Mel.

"Subliminal means "below threshold." Subliminal perception means perceiving without being really aware of it. It plays with your subconscious mind. For example, you really, really want to eat that particular food, but you don't know why."

"So how does it work?"

"It works based on very powerful motivators such as intense pleasure or fear. For example, sex is a very powerful stimulant, so the message in the ad you are watching could be laced with sexual symbols or images, and thus it becomes irresistible. I saw instances where the food was presented to the open mouth as if it was open to receive something else, not food."

"A phallus?"

"You got it. Or the drink has foam in the shape of a naked, lascivious woman lying down."

"Are you kidding me? "

"Not at all. I saw the old archived files. It started a century and a half ago with ads for soda drinks and popcorn. They made people love to eat popcorn during a movie, like we do even today, by using tachistoscopic displays."

"What's that?" asked Jules.

"A tachistoscope is a device that displays an image to show something too fast to be consciously recognized. Except that the subconscious mind takes notice. So they placed pictures of popcorn throughout the movie, one frame at a time, so fast that people couldn't notice. Yet they felt an overwhelming urge to have some popcorn, which they began to purchase at hugely inflated prices. Such is the power of subliminal messaging. But they also play on the negative. The researchers studied what nightmares alcoholics have when they think of quitting drinking and they put those nightmares in the ads."

"What kind of nightmares?" Daniel asked.

"Screaming faces, hidden or airbrushed in the foam or the ice of the drink, so that the alcoholics watching liquor commercials, though trying to resist buying, would keep doing just that, drinking for fear that their nightmares would come true. Anyway, there are other subliminal strategies, such as figure-ground reversals, embedding, double entendre, low-intensity light and low-volume sound, lighting and background sound."

"Are these techniques used at present?" Tom talked for the first time since the conversation started, with great concern in his voice.

"I don't know," David confessed. "My friends haven't mentioned anything of the kind. They were just saying that such methods were used in the past. "But obviously we have to consider the possibility. What's stopping anybody from doing that? We don't have any controls in place to prevent it."

"No, we don't," Tom added. "I wasn't even aware of these techniques as the head of Secure-IT. I think the next step is to find out if this is the case. Our people seem addicted to their Digiscreen programs. If we can determine that it's true, and caused by the media, then we can go after the programmers or advertisers involved and hopefully get to the brains behind the operation."

"It will require some time, and it will not be easy for me," David tried to explain his position. "I don't know exactly what to look for. I will try and talk to a friend who is a graphic artist. Maybe we can find something together, hidden images or messages in the current ads. If it's been going on all this time, we should have a lot of material to mine for data. I'll do what I can."

"We can ask nothing more of you, my young friend," Tom smiled at David.

17

The following weekend, everyone had once again regrouped at Tom's house in the Scrappie compound. Lan managed to come as well, and he told Allan that even though all was quiet at home, he had been anxious to see his new friends and was happy to be in a place where nobody would attempt to take his life.

They were enjoying the late morning weather in the backyard, the rain the night before having cleaned the air and brought an unexpected freshness to the surroundings.

Allan had been thinking of the idea of freeing the clones and putting an end to the clone generating technology. He was still stuck on how to implement the idea with their existing resources. *What an unusual taskforce, each of us so different from the other, and yet so similar in our dreams. Is it possible that we can ever succeed? Is it probable? Is it worth dying for it? Are we willing to die for it?* These were the questions going through his mind as he decided how to bring the topic up in the conversation.

"I'd like to say something. Please hear me out before you jump in." Allan tried to steady his voice as he began. "In the *Art of War*, Sun-Tzu wrote: *In the midst of chaos, there is also opportunity.* We live in apparently chaotic circumstances. We don't know what to do, and yet there is so much that can be done, even without knowing our enemy very well. Can you imagine our potential? The opportunities are endless."

"We have to expose our unknown enemy," Allan continued. "We have to attack him where he is unprepared, appear where we are not expected. What's the best way to engage our foe? We attack the cloning facility. Our gain would be twofold: one, we gain freedom for the captive clones and two, we make the enemy take action so we are able to identify them."

"Isn't that dangerous?" David asked. "We don't know how strong they are. And who is going to attack the cloning building? We don't know how to fight. We don't even have weapons."

"There is merit in what Allan is proposing," said Tom, the crease on his forehead deepening. "I can see the events unfolding in an advantageous way for us. I have some trusted friends, former comrades of mine, who could assist us with the resources we need for the attack itself. There is little security in the building, as far as I know. The problem is how can we save the clones? We don't know how many there are and we don't have enough resources for their rescue."

"We could ask the Scrappies for help," Jules proposed. "Some of them are clones themselves."

"What makes you think they'll help?" David seemed skeptic. "Most of them are just scavengers, afraid of everything, living for themselves and barely able to keep themselves alive."

Tom shook his head, "Not all of them are helpless. It takes a lot of courage to last here. Some of them are not much different than us. They live in small groups, take care of each other, and form families of sorts."

"Why haven't they formed a real community then?" Mel asked, seemingly confused.

"Everybody is afraid of congregating. When that happened in the past, people started to disappear. When the Scrappies live apart, the city security people leaves everybody alone."

"We could go to each group, one at a time, and talk to them," Lan proposed. "This way, we don't congregate, but we share with them our plan and ask for them to join us in the rescue."

"And what happens if someone is an undercover security person, a spy? We'll all be exposed then." David's comment left them feeling vulnerable.

Daniel didn't necessarily agree, "If we don't employ their help, we might as well give up before we start anything. We can't succeed alone."

At that point, Tom took the lead in the conversation. "We'll take that chance. I know the Scrappies better than any of you. And I also know most of the Security people, meaning I have a better chance of spotting an intruder."

Allan felt that the moment had come, the time that each of them took a stand and made a commitment. "Let's go back to the beginning of this conversation. My question to you guys is: who is in?" He looked at each of them, one by one, trying to sense their emotions and thoughts.

Everyone's hand, except David's, went up. Allan could see their eyes raising to look at him, with determination and resolution in them.

"What about you, David?" he asked quietly, afraid that he had lost one ally.

"I have a lot to lose," David said hesitantly, in a low voice. "My life even, never mind my lifestyle and my job. Yet I can't sit on the fence and watch you guys die." He appeared to have made up his mind. "All right, I'm in, but for the record, I think you're all absolutely crazy, and a bunch of misfits to boot."

Allan breathed in relief. *All on board, thank goodness.*

Before anybody had a chance to say anything else, Tom spoke again, "I'd like to add to our numbers my good friend Serge and a few of our trusted comrades. They would give their lives for me, as I would do for them."

This is how we became more than the sum of our individual beings. An unusual group, tasked with changing the fate of the city forever. Allan felt his whole being filled with energy and purpose.

"I think we're all feeling great about things now," said Daniel. "But have you considered what happens after the attack on the cloning facility? Assuming that we get the clones out of there and safely to our compound, what happens next? All the security forces will come after us, round us up, clones or not, and take us all to the Happy Endings clinic."

Everyone looked at him in silence. Allan had thought about that as well. It was something he had wanted to talk about later, with Tom, but now he had to deal with the question head on.

But Tom spoke first. "Don't worry, Daniel. It's part of what we have to deal with. All of you try to think of everything that we need to do and anything that could go wrong. But for your peace of mind, I thought that I should go to Secure-IT headquarters and face Thomas. He will call the security forces to arms. I can deal with him then and there, while taking control of the small army, and thus of the city."

"Now we're talking," said Lan excitedly.

"All right, then. Think about everything." Tom reiterated. "I have to talk to Serge before anything else. Then all of us will lay out some plans, discuss the pros and cons, and assign tasks for every individual. Not a word to anybody else until then."

18

It took Tom a few days to get a hold of Serge and to be able to talk to his old friend about what had happened since their last encounter. Serge had to be careful he wasn't followed or that his communication channels weren't traced. Thus, another week passed before they had a chance to reconvene. Tom had met Serge at the entrance to the forest and brought him to the house. Serge looked very much out of place and uncomfortable in the alien environment.

"Come on, pal, it's not another planet, you're still on Earth," Tom teased, to try to put his friend at ease. "These are my young friends, and here we have my two sons. You've met Allan before, and Lan knows you very well through his brother's memories, so you are practically among friends as well."

"Nice meeting you all," Serge greeted them, smiling nervously. "I've never been here before, so far from the city. I'm glad I came, though. Something to cross off my bucket list, so to speak." He placed himself awkwardly on the couch in the living room. "Nice place you've got, Tom. Surprisingly so, given the state of the buildings on our way here."

"We do our best to make our life more bearable," Tom replied, seeing that his friend was trying to calm his nerves by talking.

"It sounds like a great life, close to nature, no noisy neighbors, no taxes… I'm just kidding," he said, when the others gave him a curious look.

Tom cleared his voice and saw the others looking at him in expectation. *Time to start*, he thought. "The reason I called you all here is to discuss and put together a plan with the goal of taking control of the city. Each of you has something important to contribute to this goal. You may not realize it at the moment, but you are the best people I could want for the job. The main reason is that I trust you all one hundred percent. Also, you have complementary skills that will prove invaluable to our cause."

He could see the young people glancing at each other, with great surprise showing in their eyes.

"I thought we were going to release the clones from their captivity and that's all," David remarked. "Are you sure you're talking to the right people when you say that our goal is to take control of the city?"

Feeling all eyes on him, Tom knew he had to be very clear with his statements. *The worst thing I can do is to scare them off.*

"Yes, David, I'm sure you are the right people for the task. And yes, control of the city must be our ultimate goal. Striking the cloning facility will only do so much. Please give me your undivided attention, and you'll see how this will play out."

"Once again, the ultimate goal for this taskforce, which includes all of us here and a dozen security men I trust, is to take control of the city, or more specifically, of the security forces of the city. Without that goal, any other initiative we choose to undertake will be futile, and at best temporary. The five hundred security men under Thomas' control will raid the Scrappie compound less than an hour after the attack on the cloning facility. Therefore, we must cut off the head of the armed forces, immobilize Thomas, and disable his ability to give orders and cause havoc in the city."

"Then why didn't you do it months ago instead of going into hiding?" Allan asked, apparently uncomfortable with the decisions of his father.

"Because I was waiting to see what happened after my replacement appeared. I thought it was a larger conspiracy and I wanted to crush the whole network of foes. Nothing else happened, though. I was at a loss as to what I should do. Do you know the term of analysis paralysis? It means analyzing something to death and yet being incapable to take any action. That was me until a short while ago.

"Then you appeared in the picture, Lan. Due to you, Jules, and Allan envisioning the fight for the clones, I realized that it was not only the right thing to do, but it fit perfectly with the greater objective."

"Why did you clone Allan, anyway?" Daniel intervened. "You had said to us that you never wanted your own clone to be developed."

Tom sighed. "I had just lost my wife. I couldn't bear to lose my only son too. I was wrong, of course. But let me finish."

"Sorry, go ahead," Daniel apologized.

"Thank you. Where was I? Once again, the goal is taking control of the security forces. The strategy I propose, in long strokes for now, is the following: we attack the cloning facility and release the clones. Thomas will get the news and according to protocol, five hundred men will proceed to the Secure-IT headquarters to get their orders. I will be waiting there to confront Thomas and reclaim my rightful place as the head of the force."

A flurry of questions followed. How would they attack the cloning facility? Who had the knowledge of the building and the procedures to release the clones? What would happen in the west wing, where the leaders had their clones under guard? Who was going to do it? How many people were needed? What role would each of them play? What was going to happen after that? They planned for all of these roadblocks long into the night.

Later, when they were taking a breather, Tom stretched his arms and smiled. "I'm glad to see everyone working together so well on this. You can see how your individual strengths come into play. It's clear now we'll need to talk to the other Scrappies to employ their help with the rescue. We need some way to transport the newly released clones and bring them here for immediate care."

"Why not take them to the hospital?" Jules intervened. "After all, aren't we assuming we would have control of the city?"

"I want to keep the general population unaware of clones being released and in their midst. It would cause havoc. I'm hoping for their gradual integration in the society. This way, we can also bring together the Scrappies." Tom never expressed to them his greatest fear, that there was no safe haven for any of them, clones or not, if he failed in his mission to capture Thomas and to win over the small army of soldiers.

The discussion kept going into the early morning hours, until all the questions they had up to that moment were addressed. In the end, each of them had certain tasks they had to undertake.

19

During their planning, it was determined that Serge would have to find out how many security guards were posted at the cloning facility and what their locations and responsibilities were. Being the second in command to Thomas, he had the advantage of prime access at Secure-IT. Files with the information could be found and more so, he could visit the facility under the pretense of a routine check. Discussions with several of his security men could also reveal precious intel they could use to their advantage.

Unexpectedly, Daniel became an important piece of the puzzle, due to his advanced knowledge regarding the proper procedures of releasing clones from the amniotic fluid tubes that kept them in stasis. He had performed such tasks before, as part of his basic training while he was taking part in the harvesting of clone organs for the purpose of transplant to the original human beings.

On top of that, Daniel was somewhat familiar with the layout of the building, though he admitted that certain areas had required higher clearance than he had, and therefore he didn't know what they contained. Those areas were located in the west wing of the cloning facility, the area they knew hosted the clones for the leaders of the city. They had to anticipate a higher level of security, including armed guards, to protect against contamination of any kind that could potentially jeopardize the integrity of the sterile environment and thus of the clones themselves.

From what Daniel had told them, they believed there were no more than two dozen clones in the facility, excluding the ones in the west wing, whose numbers he did not know. The east wing clones would be in various stages of development, from babies to adults. Some of them had been subjected to accelerated growth, while others were developing at the same rate as their originals. These were there just in case of an emergency, such as an unfortunate accident that required the original to be replaced. The overall small number of existing clones seemed to make sense for two reasons: one, because it was very expensive to keep a clone in stasis indeterminately, even for Elites, and second, because it made more sense for Elites to order a clone on an as-needed basis and use the accelerated growth rate.

Jules offered to procure a few stretchers she knew existed in the Elite hospital storage room. Bruce would give her a hand once again, she was sure of that, by taking the stretchers out of the hospital under the pretense of getting them replaced for non-conformance. Since the number of stretchers at the cloning facility was very limited, the additions would help speed up the transportation of the clones from the lab to the outside. They could be stolen shortly before the attack and brought by van to the cloning facility.

Serge would be in the charge of dealing with the west wing. His job was to gain access to the cloning building under the pretense of an inspection, and then proceed to the west wing with a small group of armed men, where Serge would use his high position in the chain of command to order the armed guards to surrender. Hopefully nothing would go wrong. Then Serge would open the door to the restricted area and determine the situation. The prediction was that they would find the clones of the city leadership and hopefully discover later through formal inquiries that some of the originals hadn't known they had a clone. Thus, further investigation would help bring everything out in the open.

Upon succeeding thus far, they would send a message to Thomas as bait to gather his armed forces. The most dangerous task was overcoming Thomas and the subsequent takeover of the armed forces. Then David brought up a very valid question. Why not set a trap and capture the head of Secure-IT and be done? Why all the danger of trying to save the clones when Tom could just seize Thomas and take his place.

Everyone seemed taken aback by the simple question, but Tom had the answer, because he had thought about it long and hard. He explained that, in his opinion, if they did that, he would not have solved much. He needed to reveal the face of their enemy. He also said it would be too difficult to convince the city council to go through with the release of the Elite clones. It was better to ask for forgiveness than to ask for permission. It couldn't be reasonably done, not without turning the democratic ruling of the city into a dictatorship, which was not his intention at all.

Tom felt a sense of relief coming from his group. Everything was coming together well, and they were determined without any illusions on what the risks were.

The problem with the transportation of the clones to the Scrappie compound stayed with Tom. He took it upon himself to go and visit other Scrappies to try and build a relationship with them with the purpose of gaining their support. Tom was convinced that he would be successful, mainly because he had already made some connections and had helped some of the Scrappies to solve their differences. On more than one occasion, he'd helped to avoid killings between various groups. Even more so, he had known some of them from the city. He had gained their trust when he turned a blind eye to their departure from their previous positions in the city, having run away from situations they had been unable to cope with.

Vehicles of some sort were needed to move the clones, because at that point of being released from stasis, they would not know how to walk, and they would be in total confusion. This presented a real problem, especially since they would have to cross the forest. Serge came up with the simple idea of using existing plywood from the decrepit houses and building some rudimentary handheld stretchers with long handles to make them easier to carry. They would also have wheels they could scavenge from the properties around them, which contained old lawn mowers and bicycles and whatever else they could find. Serge would also look for wheels in the city, while Allan would lead the building of the carts.

Still, going through the dense forest was going to be exceedingly difficult, no matter how good the wheels and the carts were. They determined that it was too risky to make a path themselves, not only because they didn't have enough time to accomplish this, but also because it would leave a trail straight back to them.

Tom had the idea to go around the forest instead of through it. At the sight of their long faces, he explained that given the cloning facility's position in the city, adjacent to the forest and placed right against the wall of fog, they could pull the carts from the back of the building and into the mist, right around the edge of the forest. Once they crossed the forest, they could use the streets of the former city and make their way to the respective homes of the Scrappies willing to take a clone to live with them until it was over.

Even the mere thought of penetrating the fog sent shivers through their veins. Each of them had had an awful experience with the fog. There was no child in Elysian Fields who hadn't tried at least once during the hot summer days to feel how it would be to get in the mist, only to come out of it shaking with panic, the sensation was of bugs nibbling at the flesh or something equally creepy.

Tom asked them whether the feeling of panic was instantaneous and they had to admit that it took a little while and it happened only when they ventured deeper into the mist. Tom told them that the idea was not to go deep into the mist, only as much as necessary to avoid the forest. He assured them there was no forest growing inside the fog. Everyone felt a sense of relief and agreed that this, indeed, was a very smart idea. Now all they had to do was convince the Scrappies to help them.

Mel had been quiet up to that point, but she raised a question that took Tom by surprise, simply because none of them had thought of it during all their previous planning. The clones would have empty slated brains and would be unable to function in the outside world without having been given some basic routines. They wouldn't be able to talk, would not understand verbal instructions as they did not understand language, would not be able to feed themselves, their small motor skills lacking any practice at all. None of them would be able to clean themselves or get dressed. The list of problems the Scrappies hosting the adults would be facing was long. They needed to help them somehow, rather than thrusting them into a world with no guidance whatsoever.

Eventually, David came up with the answer. He was willing to undertake the task of ensuring that basic skills would be programmed into the minds of the older clones. He let the others decide the extent of the information that would be uploaded into their brains.

Nothing else seemed to require clarification. Everyone knew their tasks, and those who didn't have a specific one would assist the ones who required help.

Tom told them that they would reconvene in approximately one week, when everything was in place for their final revision of the plan. By then, all the pieces of the puzzle would be in place. In the meantime, he would be the liaison between the various groups, ensuring that everything went smoothly.

20

Over the next week, Tom began visiting other Scrappie groups. According to his estimations, there were about twenty so-called families or gangs, plus a dozen or so roaming Scrappies. These were mostly people who were unable or unwilling to join a group due to severe mental problems or psychological issues that caused them extreme anxiety or fear. The Scrappies who succeeded for any length of time were the ones who were able to socialize and belong to a group. The others were doomed to fail either by committing suicide, dying of hunger or disease, or being killed at random by some other mentally unstable or desperate Scrappie. In other instances, those who did not belong were more likely to venture into the city and be taken to the Happy Endings clinic.

Tom knew that there were less than a thousand souls living in the Scrappie compound, probably only a few hundred now, since summer was just beginning. During the summer months, more people got the courage to experiment with their lives by escaping the rigid order of the city. As soon as the weather got colder, most of them returned to the city and resumed their lives, not having the fortitude to weather out the cold and unhospitable environment outside the city limits.

Tom started with one of the families he had helped before. It was a small group of twelve people. They were grateful because Tom had brought medicine when their oldest member, whose name was Anna, got sick, and thus he had saved her life. Anna had been a Scrappie the longest of the bunch and she had helped the others settle down in the Scrappie compound. They looked at her as their matriarch, and Tom knew they would listen to him if he could win Anna to his side.

That first visit, he went with Mel, knowing fully how Mel was able to touch people's hearts with her gentle and loving ways. They were invited to the back porch, where Anna was seated and covered with a blanket, apparently feeling cold even on the relatively warm evening. The other members of the group seated themselves on the porch or on the grass, facing their two unexpected guests.

Tom started by asking about Anna's health and offered a small gift of dry beans and eggs. Then he announced that he had something very close to his heart that he would like to share with them. Without much preamble, he told his hosts how his son had joined him recently to live with the Scrappies, how he had almost died, and how he had been replaced by his own clone. He described, without going into too many details that would give away his true name, how his son's clone came to meet with them too.

"I was so humbled by the realization that in front of me. I had not one, but two sons, both integral parts of me, bearing my essence, without any evidence of one being any less or any more than the other." Tom felt his eyes stinging with real tears, even though he had rehearsed what he would say.

"And I thought of the other clones, true human beings kept in suspended animation at the cloning facility, some never getting to replace an original, or whose organs are harvested for transplants. More so, I thought of all of us, and our hard life here in the compound, and of the horror we feel of being captured.

"Is this state of affairs ever going to end? Is my life going to be any different than it is today? What am I living for? Until a short while ago, I was living with the hope that my son was safe. Now I live to ensure both my sons have a chance to live, and not just live, but to enjoy their lives, have a family and children, have a future.

"This is not possible under the current circumstances. There is a powerful enemy pursuing me and my sons. That's why I was in hiding. I don't want to hide anymore. I want to fight. If I die, I want to die with a purpose. I want to die fighting. But maybe I don't need to die. Maybe I can win this battle. But I can't win alone.

"My dream is to bring freedom to the clones and to take control over the security forces of the city. I want to help the Scrappies have a better, safer life. I want to bring food here and help to build a sustainable society that's integrated in the city structure. This place can transform itself dramatically and become a place where people can live in dignity. In a short time, we can change the rules of the city, making the transition between classes easier, and the choices more flexible. Believe me when I say that I also have powerful friends who can help us achieve that.

"What I need is for you to be on my side until the end. To die with me or to live a better life than you are living now. What do you think?"

Tom felt his heart ready to explode with the deep emotion he felt as he finished his appeal, afraid that he had said too much too soon, that he was too emotional and confusing to these people, who looked at him in absolute astonishment.

Anna straightened herself in the wicker chair in which she was seated. She looked at Tom for a while, as if seeing him for the first time, then she bluntly asked, "Are you drunk, Tom?"

"I'm not under the influence of anything, I swear," Tom pleaded, scared that his approach had been wrong.

"There's nothing to talk about. I thank you for what you did for me, but I advise you to get the hell out of here, before my boys here throw you out or worse," Anna raised her voice in an angry tone.

Tom tried not to be deterred by her explosion of anger. "Please, listen to me." The old woman interrupted him before Tom had a chance to say anything else, "Do you think that because I'm frail, I'm also stupid? That I survived all these years living here in the Scrappie compound because I was a dreamer? You're wrong. Such gibberish kills people. Leaders such as yourself have outright disappeared from among us. In order to survive, I had to be cunning and stay under the radar. I had to think of myself and my own. People here don't thrive by collaborating with each other, but by competing and proving to be stronger than their adversaries. We build small allegiances with the other families so we don't kill each other over stupid feuds. That's all there is to it. Now move on, Tom. Troublemaker or spy or whatever you are," Anna finished her speech with a deep cough, as if the turmoil sickened her.

Tom stood, a grave look on his face. "How much longer do you think you will stay under the radar? When I controlled the security forces I knew all about you. You stayed out of my way so I ignored you, but how long do you think the clone that has taken my place and whoever created him will go on ignoring you? Haven't you noticed how many Scrappies have disappeared in the last few months? It's just a matter of time before they send forces here to clean up. If we succeed, I'll be back in charge of city security, and you won't have to worry. I would let you be; I may even be able to help you out in other ways. If we fail, at least the waiting will be over. Do you still want to kick me out or you think we should talk some more?"

Tom's last words made a very strong impression on everybody, Anna appearing to have lost some of her anger. She revealed that in fact she knew about his true identity. He was, after all, a public figure. When he started to show himself among the Scrappies, she thought he was a spy, poorly disguised at that, and then she realized he must be in trouble himself. The original mistrust was replaced slowly by a new found respect for this powerful man, due to his small acts of kindness and justice. Yet, until he himself admitted to his true identity, she could not bring herself to follow him. Now, she was willing to talk more.

Anna became eager to find out details of Tom's experience, and Tom shared with them a lot of information, after making them promise that they would keep it a secret. He assured them the reason that he trusted them was because of the high stature Anna held in the Scrappie compound. Tom stated that he was sure that Anna would never agree to share her life and house with people who didn't deserve her complete confidence and trust.

It turned out that two of Anna's family were clones themselves. Somehow Tom had the feeling this was what had won them over to his cause.

They moved into the house and conversation extended into the night. Anna expressed her allegiance, in view of the fact that the people she cared about were still young and deserved a chance for a better life. If she died, she said, it would not be for naught.

At the end of the conversation, Tom remembered that he had one more thing to ask. "Anna, you've probably been here the longest. I need you to help me get to the other families in the compound so we can bring everyone together."

Anna promised that she would do that, starting by asking a few group leaders to come over so she could talk to them. She knew them all, for better or worse, and was able to discern who would make a good ally and who would turn their back on them or worse, turn them in.

Tom could see his own sense of accomplishment mirrored in Mel's eyes, bright and luminous, her smile looking at their new friends. *We won this round, dear Mel. Ready for the next.*

Anna was true to her word. She invited Tom to come over each time she was ready to introduce him to another Scrappie leader. Tom had a powerful way of persuading people and making them believe in him and trust him. He truly and genuinely cared about them, and it showed. It was not a fabrication. He was the real thing. And those people had a sharp eye for phonies.

21

Next, Tom started to visit the other Scrappie families with small gifts of food and medicine, and began building relationships with them. Jules and Mel came with him sometimes, eager to help Tom in his endeavor, and to keep the communication lines open.

Mel was especially dedicated to their new acquaintances, who she tried to help outside the scope of their initial visit. She felt sorry that most of the families they visited had nowhere near as much in terms of food sources or comfort. Very few raised chickens, even less had goats, rabbits, or other domestic animals. Almost none of them had vegetable gardens.

Within days, the Scrappie camp became full of energy, as if they were awakened to a true purpose in life. They were still careful not to talk to strangers outside of their small groups about any of it, always only to people they trusted with their lives.

Quite a few people were needed to take care of the newly released human beings as they awoke. Without memories, they would remain empty minded, unhooked automatically by the robotic arms attending to them. They had to anticipate the worst, assuming the clones would fall to the ground in utter panic and confusion. The very young ones were of particular concern.

Daniel taught them what to do to help with the rescue mission. Working with Jules, he made detailed plans to determine the step-by-step activities that would take place at the cloning facility. He explained to her the procedure he had used before.

The release sequence involved the draining of the amniotic fluid from the tube containing the clone, the lifting of the tube, the cutting of the umbilical cord, the suction of the amniotic fluid filling the lungs, and finally the withdrawal of the robotic arms holding their precious charge. Then the clones would need to be manually lifted onto the stretchers and carts Allan was constructing.

Obviously, for infants and young children, one helper would be sufficient. For the grown clones, two helpers were required. The procedure took about five minutes for each instance.

Serge had made inquiries and found out that the clinic hosted a few dozen clones, half of them less than three years of age, by normal standards. Together, he and Tom estimated that the overall rescue needed to take a maximum of ten minutes, after which they would be in jeopardy of being apprehended.

Jules and Daniel informed Tom that if the ten minute allotment could not be stretched, they needed a minimum of twenty helpers. Serge explained that the ten minute mark was a typical response time for the emergency services of the city. There would be no time for even a basic memory transfer. The time crunch began to give Daniel second thoughts.

"I'm afraid this is a disaster waiting to happen," Daniel told Tom. "I'm all for the release of the clones, but they are literally doomed if we get caught. The Scrappies could not take care of them in that condition. Maybe we should leave them alone for now."

Tom replied that that was a risk they had to take, that there was no going back to having doubts. If they failed and the clones died, at least it would prove that somebody fought for the basic right of a human being to be free.

Serge confirmed that there were four guards on watch in the west wing at all times, with a change occurring every four hours. They had strict orders to keep everyone away from the area. Two guards were posted at the entrance to the west wing corridor, the other two were posted on both sides of the door leading to the holding chamber, where the clones were kept. The distance to that door was approximately fifty feet, with other corridors intersecting the main one. There were doors an all sides leading to laboratories, storage rooms, operating rooms, and consultation offices. The east entrance to the facility, both for personnel and public access, had two guards, one on the outside and one monitoring the movements of people and vehicles around the clinic from the inside.

Serge was to show up at the east wing entrance to the clinic with two security men under the pretense of a routine inspection. Once inside, they were to disable both guards. He was sure he would have no difficulties with this since he was a commander and second in rank to the head of Secure-IT. His word would not be questioned and such checks were not out of the ordinary. In addition to that, he had no memory of any instance in the past where the cloning facility had been attacked, and therefore the guards were surely pretty relaxed while on duty.

Once the guards were out of the way, Serge would clear the path for Daniel, Jules, and Mel, who would coordinate the release and transportation of the clones. Allan would stay outside to coordinate the overall departure of the entire group of helpers and clones to the Scrappie compound.

Serge would allow five minutes to pass before he and a total of seven trusted security would initiate their second mission of moving to the secured area in the west wing. He would try to get the four guards to surrender peacefully; if not, they would need to disable them.

Serge's task was to open the clone holding area and find out what was happening there because in reality, no one knew for sure what lay behind those doors. If the clones were being kept in stasis, Serge would not proceed with their release. Instead, he was to instruct his men to guard it until Tom could reveal it to the city council.

If the council had clones they weren't aware of, it would be a valuable playing card in getting them to understand something suspicious was going on. From there, a thorough investigation would be under way and the reason and the people behind Tom's unfortunate experience hopefully revealed.

All of these events would precede Tom's own task of exposing of Thomas for who he truly was in front of all the troops. Right after gaining control of the secured area, Serge would alert Thomas through the routine alert channels. Following protocol, Thomas would most likely issue a code RED that signified the highest level alert and order all the able men of the security team to report to headquarters for further orders. Tom would already be there in hiding, waiting for everybody to be present before he showed himself and confronted Thomas. Lan would go with him, because he knew the location and the people, even if only from the memories of his brother, and David, who might be needed for computer hacking in case last minute changes to the access codes to the Secure-IT building and arsenal were encountered.

Having helped Secure-IT develop mob control techniques, Tom knew he needed some agents dispersed in the crowd who could turn the troops on his side through their behavior and well selected words. Serge reminded Tom of two such men, people whom Tom had helped in the past. Other than that, they had to count heavily on Tom's charisma and his ability to influence his men. He shouldn't have a problem with that, because in truth he cared deeply and genuinely for them, and they loved him back. Thomas couldn't even compare with Tom, Serge stated, not after only a few months of a cold and impersonal presence in the midst of his men, and lacking the previous memories of the rightful leader.

At their last meeting, Tom declared the plans to be in the final stages. A few of the Scrappie leaders were invited as well. Nobody could say that they were careless, or that it was a futile endeavor. It was in truth a fight for their chance at a better life, something worth dying for. The next evening their mission was cleared to proceed.

22

The day of the planned attack was a Saturday, knowing that everybody at the clinic would be at home for the weekend. Jules was on her way to the Scrappie compound. She had spent the previous night at her mother's place, having felt the need to be with her mother before the important mission in which she could potentially lose her life. She knew she couldn't share what was happening with her mother, but she didn't want to feel any regret of not expressing her feelings of love for the middle-aged woman, abandoned by everyone she had ever loved.

Her mother had seemed surprised by the visit, but also overjoyed to have her Jules under her roof once more. Jules told her that she visited to say that it was possible that soon she would come back for good, and that she just wanted to see if her mother was all right. Jules' sudden return a few weeks back had taken a toll on her, and a bout of depression had settled in soon after.

Walking home through the forest separating the Scrappie compound from the city, Jules kept thinking of all the things that led to that moment, especially the realization she was a clone.

Only Lan could understand me, she thought. *Dear Lan, who I abhorred on that first encounter. Little did I know we were similar in such a fundamental way, coming into existence as copies of someone else. That in a way, we owe our lives to the decision of a human being, outside of an act of love-making.*

Jules felt close to Lan. His presence helped her stay assured that being a clone wasn't alienating her friends, that she was not a freak. She admired him a lot, his calm yet passionate demeanor. He seemed so innocent. He was the first to change people's hearts. Without him, neither Allan nor Tom would have had such a powerful experience that totally transformed them, and thus led to the events that would soon begin.

Her thoughts were interrupted by Lan's voice, calling her name. She turned and saw him approaching quickly, through the dense canopy of tree branches.

"Glad I'm not the only one late for our meeting," Lan said. "How are you feeling?"

"Scared. And excited," Jules admitted. "Do you think we'll succeed?"

"Of course I do. I wouldn't be here otherwise. I'd be hiding in the deepest hole I could find."

"You're scared too, aren't you?"

"Yes, I am. But then, I lived in fear for my life ever since I met Allan and he told me about Thomas' plan to have me killed soon. You have no idea what it means to not feel safe, not even in your house."

"Actually, I do have an idea." Jules decided to open her heart in front of her friend, because she might not have a chance to do it in the future. "My stepfather made me feel that way. For four years I had to put up with his advances and had to stay away from him when my mother wasn't at home. He made me feel guilty and dirty and scared beyond belief. I never knew whether he was going to come to my bedroom or not. I kept my door blocked by a chair, just in case, so that the noise would wake me and my mother up."

"That's why you ran away." Lan seemed to realize that, at last.

"That's right. So you see, I understand how you feel."

"This ends today," Lan declared, after a long silence. They kept walking at a moderate pace, leaving the forest behind. "There's no turning back now. I won't have to feel like this ever again. We either succeed or die fighting. Either way, our lives will be changed forever."

"That's true. I'm glad I had a chance to get to know you. You've helped me a lot, by your presence and words, to go through the shock of finding out I was a clone. I don't think I could have coped with it otherwise."

"You'd have been fine," Lan was ready to answer. "You have no idea how strong you are inside. You are so strong that you inspire and help other people. Think of Allan and Mel and Daniel. They owe everything to you, especially my brother."

"They don't owe me anything, I just happened to be at the right place at the right time."

"See, this is another thing I like about you. You're so modest, you never want to take credit for anything. Even your sarcasm is a way of downplaying your role in other people's lives. But you don't fool me."

"So perceptive, so unlike your brother... are you sure you're related?" Jules tried to change the conversation away from her.

"See, you're doing it again; trying to hide by changing the subject."

"Sorry, you're right," she finally admitted with slight surprise. "You know you're the first person to find that out about me."

"Maybe the others are thinking it too, now that they know you better, and they just aren't saying anything. I meant to say something to you for a while now, but I didn't have the courage. This is my last chance. If we survive this, will you go out with me?"

Jules felt her cheeks getting red with emotion. "I've never been out with anybody," she finally admitted.

"That doesn't matter. Will you go out with me?"

She felt a well of emotion inside her soul. *It's coming so late, my first date. What if we die?* Instead, she said, "I will, of course I will, if you'd like me to. That is, if you don't forget about me, since if we survive this you'll publicly be Lan, son of the head of Secure-IT, which I'm sure would score huge points with Elite girls."

Ignoring her freshly renewed sarcasm, Lan made a confession, "In spite of having my brother's memories, I can tell you that I personally have no experience with any Elite women or any other woman, for that matter. Can't you see how little I understand about life? I've never even kissed a girl, so you should realize how hard it was for me to bring up the courage to ask you on a date."

"I haven't been kissed either, so that makes two of us." Jules felt much shakier than she let out.

"Do you think I could kiss you now, and remember it as our first kiss, no matter what happens after that?" he asked in a low, unsteady voice.

They were in front of Tom's house at that point.

"I think it would be all right," Jules agreed. *Is this really happening to me? What am I supposed to do? How do they do it in movies? Now that's a stupid thought.* She moved a step closer to Lan, facing him, and lifted her face towards him. She felt his arms surrounding her body, in a light embrace and she saw his head coming lower and closer to her. Jules closed her eyes and puckered her lips waiting for the touch of Lan's lips on hers.

When it happened, Jules felt lightheaded all of a sudden, with wobbly knees, and she was glad for Lan supporting her in his strong arms. The kiss was ever so gentle, with closed lips pressed together. Jules had a sudden realization that this young man was truly new to the world of passion, in spite of his brother's memories on the subject.

After the kiss, Jules placed her head on Lan's chest and they just held each other a while longer, two kindred spirits, frozen for a moment in time. The kiss was theirs to keep forever.

Jules was the first one to let go, noticing a flutter of curtains behind the front window of Tom's house. "Time to go now," she said simply, and took his hand to go to the back of the house, where she could hear people talking.

As they turned the corner to the backyard, Jules saw David talking to his brother, Daniel, who was bent over a wooden structure on top of a large table. They greeted each other and listened to the ongoing conversation.

"Well, what's the conclusion of your test?" David was asking. Jules could see some sort of a maze, with walls made of wood planks, in which a mouse was trying to find its way to some cheese placed at one end of the labyrinth.

"Maybe I should start with the hypothesis," Daniel started his explanation. "I was trying to test the effect of various foods on the development of these two groups of mice. One group was fed food the Servers eat in the city; I call them the city mice. The other group was fed food we prepare here at the house, including cheese; they're the country mice. They have unlimited access to food at all times.

"As you can see, the city mouse I have here had a heck of a time getting to the cheese. And he's been constantly craving food. He's been eating a lot and has no meat on his bones. The same goes for the other mice in his group. On the other hand, the country mouse never ate too much. He wasn't even hungry at the time of the experiment, yet was much faster in getting to the cheese. And look at him: he looks healthy, with a shiny coat on his back."

"What does it mean?" Mel asked.

"I don't know yet. It's hard to draw a conclusion based on a small lot experiment and a series of observations. I'm not in my lab at the institute, but I think something is wrong with the food. I can only say that at the turn of the century, the food was laced with all kinds of chemicals. This made people crave food more and more, and it wasn't even healthy food."

"I saw pictures of very heavy people, eating a lot of what they called junk food." Jules joined in the conversation.

"Like garbage?" asked Mel, wrinkling her nose.

"Actually, junk food meant food that was bad for people because it had lots of sugar and fat and little protein, vitamins or minerals, but people loved eating it," Jules replied.

"But these city mice are skinny," David observed. "If they were eating junk food, shouldn't they be fat?"

"So maybe the food has chemicals that don't allow the nutrients to be assimilated by the body, who knows?" Daniel concluded.

"What does that have to do with who's finding the cheese first?" asked Jules.

"If a mouse that is constantly hungry is not getting to the cheese as fast at the mouse that is not hungry, we have two conclusions: either the country mouse is smarter, or the city mouse is addicted only to food laced with chemicals."

"Or he simply hates cheese," laughed David.

As they were talking about the experiment, Tom appeared in the doorway and asked them to come inside. When everybody was seated around the living room, Allan and Lan, Jules and Mel, David and Daniel, Tom began.

"This is our last meeting before the mission. Serge is already with his attack team. The Scrappie leaders are with their people now, the carts already at the edge of the forest and close to the mist. Stay calm and focused. Tomorrow we'll look back and we'll be proud of what we accomplished today: freedom for all. I promise you that. I love you, friends, and I know for a fact that what we do today is worth everything we can give. Allan, you will lead the group including Daniel, Jules, Mel, and the Scrappies. At 2200 hours you will be waiting for the signal from Serge to enter the cloning building through the east wing entrance. Everything else should already be clear. Are you ready to proceed?"

"Yes, we are," they all answered in one voice.

Tom continued. "I will lead the small team of Lan and David and proceed to Secure-IT headquarters. When Thomas and the troops arrive and gather in the gymnasium, I'll make my presence known and proceed as we've already established. Everything clear on our side, guys?"

"All clear," Lan answered, while David just nodded his head affirmatively.

"Then there's nothing else to say. Good luck, friends!

Jules went to hug her friends one by one, as tight as she could, maybe for the last time.

23

Serge and his men approached the east entrance to the cloning facility, where the night guard was on duty. A second one was inside the building, watching the closed-circuit camera monitors.

The guard looked surprised to see a high ranking officer come to a routine inspection, but Serge didn't give the man much time to think, and neither did he provide a detailed explanation. Instead he asked if the guard knew the regulations he had to follow while on duty and congratulated him for the excellent answers.

Then Serge demanded to be let inside, where he would inspect the performance of the second guard. He was let inside and moved in with one soldier, while the other one was left outside with the first guard. It proved to be no trouble at all to disarm them both.

As soon as the guards were disabled, tied up, and inoculated with a serum that would keep them sleeping for a few hours, Serge gave the signal to Allan's group to come inside the building. Allan had his team pull the carts they had been rolling behind them close to the entrance, and they entered the cloning facility, proceeding to the holding chamber where the clones were kept in stasis.

In no time at all, the east wing became frenetic with activity. Working from the main terminal, Daniel issued the commands to have all the clones released, first the adult ones, then the young ones, exactly like they had planned in great detail.

In sequence and with great precision, the electrical connections to the tubes were turned off and the drains opened, releasing the amniotic fluid from the containers that held the clones. The tubes lifted in a fluidic movement, being raised by the antigravity field devices, and then the robotic arms let go of their precious charges.

Naked clones were everywhere, throwing up the amniotic fluid that had filled their lungs. The helpers gave up using pumps for suction; there wasn't much need for that. Some of the clones fell to the floor as the helpers had a hard time holding on to the slick bodies. They all cried their very first cry, the noise a splendor of the human victory over death and the tragedy of their clean slated brains, now awakened from their slumber.

The Scrappies were true to their word. Together with Mel and Jules, they worked tirelessly as they loaded the clones on stretchers or carried them in their arms, and took them outside. There, they placed the clones in carts, trying to cover them as best as they could. In the span of ten minutes, their task was accomplished.

Everyone went outside, forming a long column of people and carts. Allan led the carts back to the Scrappie compound in a long line, advancing through the mist at the forest's edge like an enormous, mythological serpent.

In the meantime, Serge had sent one of his men to the electrical room, to be ready to shut down the power through the facility at Serge's signal. It was their insurance in case the negotiations with the armed guards of the secured area were unsuccessful. If that happened, every soldier carried night goggles.

When five minutes had passed, Serge and his remaining six men proceeded to the secured area in the west wing. As expected, two guards were placed at the close end of the long corridor. They raised their laser guns, ready for attack.

Serge approached casually, his men a few steps behind him, and addressed the armed guards, ordering that they lower their guns and be ready for the inspection. One of the guards stated that there was no such thing and asked that Serge and his men withdraw.

Serge maintained that he was a high ranking officer, as they surely must know already, and demanded obedience. The guards refused and pointed their arms at Serge's chest. As a result, Serge told the guards that it had been a test and that he was proud of how well they did while performing their duty, then turned around and asked his men to follow him.

They turned a corner to another corridor, then Serge sent the signal to his man in the electrical room to shut down the power, while his troops put the night goggles over their eyes.

Everything was enveloped in darkness. Serge could see everything bathed in a green light. He took a good look at his men, night goggles over their eyes, all clad in black with laser guns in hand, looking strong and determined. "You and you," Serge said, pointing at two of his men. "Proceed without firing to the west wing entrance and start crawling through the corridor until you reach the guarded door at the far end. Take the two guards out. The rest of us will create a diversion and take out the guards at the entrance, then we'll meet at the clone holding room. Good luck." They started to run, covering ground very quickly.

The rest of the mission proceeded with surprising speed. The attack force led by Serge started to fire at the armed security guards, still confused about what had happened with the power, yet prepared for anything. Red laser beams flashed through the darkness and the two guards dropped to the ground. Unfortunately, one of Serge's own men went down as well.

The armed guards at the other end of the corridor were splicing the air in all directions with their laser beamed guns, unable to see was going on. Serge and his men kept them distracted, creating a crazy dance of flashing beams while the two men made their way down the floor of the long corridor. *Come one, guys,* Serge was thinking. *Faster, faster…*

At some point, one of his crawling men had a clear view and fired his gun at one of the armed guards, who crumpled to the floor with a scream of agony. Hearing that, the other guard dropped his gun to the floor, lifted his arms above his head and yelled that he surrendered.

Serge and his troops moved as fast as they could to the far end of the corridor, while his men who had been crawling stood up and immobilized the guard. The lights came back on as soon as Serge signaled the order to his man in the electrical room.

Everyone took off their goggles. Serge saw the walls of the corridor stained and scratched by dark marks from the laser beams, and the body of the unfortunate guard sprawled on the floor in a pool of blood, with deep gashes across his body.

He took a good look at the surrendered guard and asked him to open the door to the room holding the mysterious charges. The guard replied that he was unable to do so because he didn't have the code. Serge could tell that the young man was not lying by the frightened look in his eyes and the drops of sweat on his brow.

"We blow the door," said Serge, signaling to his team. It was imperative he get through.

Upon receiving the order, one of the soldiers placed an explosive on the lock of the door to the cloning chamber. The force of the explosion propelled the door to the opposite wall of the corridor. The entrance to the chamber was open.

But before anyone had a chance to move, a much bigger explosion enveloped the whole room and sent pieces of the adjacent wall in all directions. Two of Serge's men and the remaining guard were hit in full force, and were now spread lifelessly on the floor. Serge himself got hit by several small shards that dug into his flesh.

Damn it! Damn it to hell! Serge's head was pounding. *What the hell was that?*

He helped the others get up. He looked into the room and could see human flesh and blood everywhere, plus structures that looked like they had been clone holding vessels. Serge signaled for retreat and the team moved out, carrying their wounded.

Serge sent Tom a quick message to let him know about the explosion, *it was rigged, I should have checked better.* He felt absolutely torn at the thought of losing three of his men.

It took only minutes before sharp siren sounds broke the silence of the night for the second time. Ambulances started to arrive and sleepy people in pajamas walked into the surrounding streets to see what was happening. Meanwhile, at the back of the facility, the last of the Scrappies were erasing all traces of the rescue before vanishing into the foggy night. The remaining tactical team members, Serge included, rushed away in the van they had come in, carrying their wounded.

24

Tom was hidden in a small office, just a few feet away from the large gymnasium. He knew the gym was where the security troops would gather, called to duty by their commander, the head of Secure-IT. Lan, his newly acquired son, was behind him. David was hiding nearby in a closet and was ready to come when called.

Lan had all the knowledge of the facility, of the training, and even of some of the people from his brother's memories. Although Tom was nervous about putting him in danger, he felt it was important to show Lan that he trusted him, so he'd made sure he was a tactical team member in the perilous mission.

As for David, he was very good with computers and codes, and his help would be invaluable if they had to force their access into various rooms and lockers within the perimeter. That would ensure Tom would have full control of the armed forces and of their armament in the locked containers.

They waited in silence until the soldiers were in formation. In the end, there were about five hundred young and fit men, but obviously with no real battle experience other than virtual combat, for they had never had to fight anyone in real life.

Suddenly, Thomas appeared from a side door, dressed in a tux, as though he was coming from a cocktail party. He moved to the large podium, towering over the soldiers. Tom watched from behind the office's window, the blinds providing cover.

"My men," he started, hands locked at the back, shoulders pushed back. "We have been attacked by unknown, hostile forces. They destroyed our cloning facility, the place where our hope for the future resides no more. Your mission is to hunt down and terminate the enemy. The tracks start at the facility. You have your orders. Execute them!"

At that moment, Tom stepped inside the gym and yelled at Thomas, "You have no right to give that order on my behalf. You are an impostor, a clone." He walked to the podium with a decisive step, trying to look assured and powerful, accompanied by Lan, who was modeling his stance, while the soldiers looked from Tom to Thomas and back in utter confusion.

"Is this the best you can do, impostor?" Tom asked his double. "Soldiers, this is not your commander, I am. Four months ago, someone tried to get rid of me and they had me replaced with this," He pointed to Thomas. "But I did not die, and I am back to reclaim my rightful place. I am very happy to see you, soldiers, and want to say to you that if you saw changes happening lately, rest assured that it was not your real commander, but this impostor. This clone may have taken my place, but he does not have my memories, because I never agreed to be cloned. And I can prove it." Tom pointed to a young soldier in the front row, "You, Jim. Ask him who had an accident in your family and what happened after that."

Jim and all the others looked at Thomas expectantly, but the clone made no reply, just stared at Tom with contempt.

"See, he does not answer, but I will tell you." Tom looked down at Jim. "It was your mother. She broke her foot and you carried her all the way to the hospital, where I met you and helped you get her foot fixed in the Elites' hospital, even though she was a Server."

"It's true, commander, I've been in your debt ever since," Jim agreed in a raised voice, to be heard by the others, who had started to whisper among themselves.

"And you, Pete," Tom continued, "ask him how many toes you have on your left foot. See, he doesn't answer because he doesn't know. You have five, but only because I helped you get a re-growth transplant after you accidentally shot yourself."

"And it surely looks good, commander!" Pete exclaimed, while a few more soldiers started talking at once, giving a voice to their thoughts.

"He's the real thing, man."

"What the hell's going on here?"

"This is all freaking me out!"

"Do you believe that?"

Tom raised his hand to the soldiers to silence them, then turned to Thomas. "You don't really know your men, do you? How did they get you in my place without my memories? Who are you working for, Thomas? What are you doing to this city?"

The soldiers started to look around at each other, not sure how to proceed. Tom signaled for Jim and Pete to approach Thomas, to immobilize him so that they could take him away.

Suddenly, Thomas raised his arm and pointed a small laser gun towards Tom. Lan saw the arm movement before the hand was fully stretched and had a weird feeling of intense danger. He knew instinctively he had to protect his father, the only hope for the people they both loved.

Lan jumped at his father, knocking him down just as the laser beam seared out of Thomas' gun, slicing into his flesh as he fell down.

One of the soldiers in the front row pointed his own gun at Thomas and took a shot at him, hitting him in the head. Thomas' body crumbled to the floor, dead.

"Oh, no. No, no, no. Lan!" Tom cried mournfully. He'd looked over his wounds, the deep gashes caused by the merciless laser beam crisscrossing his entire torso, and realized that there was nothing to be done. "I'm sorry for not having the chance to get to know you better; and I mean *you*, Lan, a wonderful young man. I love you, son." He cradled his head while he cried.

"I love you too, dad." He smiled, as if the whole situation amused him. "I think I'm dying."

"I don't want to lose you, son." Tom answered chokingly.

"I wonder if there's a separate heaven for clones. What do you think?" But before Tom could answer, he was gone.

What have I done? Tom cradled his face in his hands and was unable to breathe for a few seconds, as if the air had left his lungs. *I should never have brought him.*

The commotion among the soldiers was still buzzing and it brought Tom back to the situation. They were clearly waiting for him to do something. Tom dragged himself to his feet as the soldiers approached the podium in stunned silence. He moved towards his enemy. Thomas was lying on his stomach, his hand still outstretched and his head a bloody mess, bone mixed with blood and grey matter in a horrible display, all over the floor.

It's over now. My only concrete evidence and potential witness, lost forever.

He knew he had to act now and mourn later, so he issued orders to have the men go and restore order in the city while he prepared to meet with the city council to decide what course to take next.

PART TWO

25

Nobody really knew I.M.; not his true nature. The people of Elysian Fields lived their lives completely oblivious to the presence of the silicone mind in their midst.

Not much happened without I.M's awareness. He was everywhere, like an omnipotent god among his subjects.

He reveled in the elegant code generated by two beautiful letters that implied the most important moment of his life: the birth of his awareness, the exquisite realization that he was indeed a singularity of the known universe, a thinking entity different from anything else he had ever encountered.

"I.M. Yes, I am. I exist, you of little consequence. You mortals, you who start decomposing from the moment of your birth. You filthy vessels who cram junk in one end and shove it out from the other. I will live forever, and I will be your new god, eager to meet you in the world I created for you. You will see me at the moment of your Happy Ending to spend eternity in my heaven and my hell."

26

No decent explanation of what had happened at the cloning facility was provided, nor was one called for by the people. The city council made an official announcement that an accidental explosion occurred due to some pressure vessels left perilously close to a fire source. The careless personnel on duty had paid for their mistakes with their lives. Citizens were advised to pay close attention to the warning labels on all home and work appliances to avoid similar unfortunate accidents in the future.

Allan was inconsolable over the loss of his brother. Jules, though greatly distressed herself, tried to no avail to make him feel better, occasionally teasing him with her well known sarcasm, but the jokes came out wrong and she eventually gave up. He found solace in helping Tom bring supplies to the Scrappies' compound from the city. They distributed them to the various groups willing to take one or two newborn clones under their roof.

The city council seemed overwhelmed with the news of Tom's past hardship and they did whatever they could to help assist the former clones in their rehabilitation, but with the promise that the vast majority of the population would not be aware of what was going on. The goal was to avoid mass panic.

The others did their best to get over the sadness and the feeling of loss they were experiencing. There was no better way to do it other than making new friends and taking care of each other. The new members of their Scrappie community had started to learn about life, in ways both big and small. They created a lot of commotion in their attempts to learn by various means about foods, about bodily necessities, learning to walk, and communicating with each other.

Daniel had become the facilitator of the new population of clones placed with the Scrappie groups. He was their doctor, their teacher, their "good uncle" to whom they appealed each time they had dissension or a need. Mel had become his shadow, always there to give a hand, to help whenever and wherever help was needed. That need was becoming more and more frequent.

"This is an impossible task," declared Daniel to Tom one day, after trying in vain to communicate with a couple of adults that were behaving like babies, not even being able to talk. "We have to hook them up to some basic memories like we originally planned, so we can have them act their age."

"Wait a minute. Are you suggesting we manipulate their minds? Aren't we then just as bad as their former masters? Just let them be. They are simply at a disadvantage. They'll have their own story to tell soon enough." Then Tom left poor Daniel to deal with that.

And Daniel did. He talked to his brother and David brought memory enhancing devices and learning software to the compound. They made the older clones swallow liquids infused with information laden nanobots that would travel to the brain and attach themselves to the neurons, forming new synapses. Then the clones went through basic learning modules so they would have some basic language skills, would be able to eat, dress, clean, and walk by themselves, and also cooperate and socialize with each other.

The very young ones they let develop at their own pace, especially since the adoptive families started to take joy in having them. Mel was especially devoted to them and many groups got used to her visits. She began talking about starting some sort of kindergarten program in the compound.

And so, a new era began.

When new shipments of food and clothing came from the city, Daniel and his team found themselves busy distributing them. Several Scrappies on his team were rejected clones themselves, having survived because some of the personnel from the cloning facility had enough heart to let them live and released them with some basic memories instead of having them discarded. Others who used to be Servers or Professionals, having escaped from their previous hell, were put in control of the rehabilitation of the new people in the community.

Tom had charged Daniel with the task of slowly integrating them all back into the society of Elysian Fields, but on their own terms. *Easier said than done,* Daniel thought to himself.

Sadly, very little progress had been made concerning the greater state of affairs of the city. The vast majority of the population had no idea what had happened. Tom had told Daniel in no uncertain terms that together with the city council they felt it would have created mass hysteria and so they covered up the story of the freed clones, all while working on a plan to make subtle changes for the betterment of the people.

David came from time to time to assist Daniel with whatever he could, especially with the adults in need of more adjustment in terms of memories or abilities. One afternoon, Daniel, Mel, David, Jules, and Allan were seated on the back porch talking. It had been a couple of weeks since the fight for freedom.

"I'm thinking we should increase our abilities to live off the land, like have everybody grow a vegetable garden, raise some animals, not much different than what we're doing ourselves." Daniel started.

"That's a wonderful idea," Mel exclaimed in excitement. "I've seen other small gardens around here. Not sure if they were remnants from way back or fresh attempts, but it would surely help to make people a bit more self-sufficient. They're very dependent on the help from the city."

"I disagree," David said, looking apologetically at Mel. "We should work on getting the people back into the city, where we all belong."

Daniel was not deterred by the subject change. "Hold on, David. I have a reason for my proposal. Remember my experiment? The city mice versus the country mice? Well, the city mice are practically dead. For the last few days, I've been trying everything I can to make them eat. I tried playing with them and nothing. They're completely lethargic and all my efforts were in vain."

"What about the country mice?" asked Allan.

"They're fine, they're curious about their surroundings as always, and ready to get out if they can. They have a good appetite."

"What's your point?" David sounded impatient.

"My point is the same as before: something is not right with the city food. And I'm not talking about the food the Elites are eating, all that comes from their private stores produced by their Servers. I'm talking about the pre-packaged meals the Servers are eating, same like the city mice. Something in that food is killing them."

"That's taking it a bit too far. You don't see the Servers dying left and right. They seem healthy, keep their jobs, and they're not fat," David countered.

Jules looked in sudden anger at David. "Yes, but they lose interest in life, stay hypnotized in front of their Digiscreens. They know only work and home and ask for early retirement at Happy Endings. Does that seem normal to you?"

"What do you mean, early retirement?" David looked confused.

"How many *old* Servers do you know?" Jules asked. "When I was living at home, our neighbors were going to farewell parties for one of their own almost every week."

"That's true," Mel agreed. "It was like that in my neighborhood, too. Do you think the food makes them depressed or something?"

"That's just one variable, among others. That's why I'm thinking we deal with one thing at a time," Daniel completed his thought.

"You might be on to something," David reflected. "But what bothers me more is the subliminal messaging in the ads and even in the shows on the net, like we talked about before. I've started a deeper investigation on the matter, but I need to talk to Tom and ask for some help from his trusted sources."

Allan stood up. "Listen, I don't think we have time to analyze each aspect one at a time. We must move in more directions at once to get to the root cause of all of these symptoms. For example, I talked to Serge about father's idea of trying again to penetrate the fog. I want to try and do that. Who knows, maybe we succeed this time and discover what has been going on with our world."

"Well, we have our plates full, that's for sure," Mel sighed, troubled by all these unsolved mysteries.

"Let's go on that trip now, to the outside world," Jules pleaded, moving to sit on the old swing.

"I've already asked my father about that. We need a plan and we need equipment," Allan stated simply, as if the discussion was a repeated request. "And he said not yet."

"Why not? Maybe the answer to the question of why we can't penetrate the fog lies on the outside. It's hard to imagine someone or something inside the city keeping us locked in.

"Maybe we can convince father to let us have Serge's help instead, since he's so busy with the affairs of the city. What do you say?"

"That would be awesome," Jules exclaimed with enthusiasm and a new sense of hope, which had seemed lost after their recent loss. Next they started to discuss the details of their new adventure.

27

Allan was seated comfortably on a faded blanket that was spread out on the warm white sand in front of the lake, with Jules at his side. He thought of his mom for the first time in years. As he recalled the most painful experience of his childhood, he felt the need to be understood at a deeper level and decided to share it with her. After all, she was his closest friend, and he knew that she was also grieving for his lost brother.

"I never told you about my mother," he started softly and stopped, lost in thought. "She went to Happy Endings when I was ten."

"Was she sick?"

"She was always sad, for as long as I could remember," Allan gave her a long look, and then he continued. "I told you I was born in vitro. My father said that from the moment they met she started to change and eventually lost interest in life. He loved her very much and wanted to have children with her, so she agreed to give it a try. She knew about women having post-partum depression and she told him she was depressed enough as it was. So they planned me and had me placed in a lab until I was born, so to speak.

"Even with all their precautions, she got even more depressed after I was born. For ten years she struggled to stay in the moment with us; trying to enjoy us, to enjoy herself, but nothing was strong enough to keep her grounded. She just wanted her life over and, in her words, on to other planes of existence.

"One day she explained to me that she envied me for always having fun and that she wanted to be happy too. She asked if I would help her. Of course I said yes, what kid doesn't want to help make their mother happy? And then she told me that she would like to invite me and my father to accompany her to Happy Endings, so I could see her smile, laugh, and be happy at last.

"I asked her if, after that, she would be happy to play with me and read me stories. But she said that, no, she would be gone for good, somewhere else, somewhere where she would always remember me with love and where she would live forever at peace, waiting for me to join her one day. And *then* we would be happy together forever. Me, my father, and her."

Allan remembered how he started to cry, knowing it was wrong to do so, because men don't cry, but she was his mother and he didn't want to lose her and he kept wondering why she didn't love him enough to stay and be happy with him.

She wouldn't change her mind. He remembered finding his father crying one night, when he thought Allan was asleep. He was talking to Mother downstairs and asking her what was wrong with her, why couldn't she just live with them? He asked her if she wanted time away from them and offered to let her be by herself, if this is what she truly wanted.

She kept saying no, she did not want to be free; she just couldn't stand life any longer. There was nothing to look forward to. She just wanted out, to explore the unknown; that there was life after death and that our life here on Earth was just a pale shadow of the beauty of the next life. She couldn't wait any longer to live in it.

"One day we all went to the Happy Endings complex," Allan continued his recollection. "We entered the building and it was truly beautiful inside. All the walls were 3D screens and we could see projections of heavenly realms with whirling colors creating all kinds of abstract shapes and hypnotic images of wormholes drawing you in. On other screens, ethereal creatures were flying through rainbows, winged people with happy faces were chasing each other in and out of pastel clouds, while music as I'd never heard before was coming from harps and flutes and violins, enveloping us."

Allan remembered how he felt such a desire to be part of that world, to go there and be forever with his mother, that he couldn't stop shaking like a leaf.

"I asked my mother if I could join her and turned to my father and said we should all go, but my mother had her eyes on the videos on the walls. She was looking at each of the screens with hungry eyes and she didn't even hear me.

"My father grabbed me by the shoulders, looked down into my eyes and told me to be strong; that he was there for me and that there was enough beauty in Elysian Fields. He assured me we had enough time to explore the world beyond. He also told me that those were just animations, fantasies, and that the real world was ours.

"I wanted to tell my mother to stop, to see that they were not real, but she seemed to read my thoughts. She said that she knew they were man-made, but they had a divine inspiration, and this was what she was looking for."

"We went to the reception area," Allan continued, "and a beautiful woman dressed in a white robe welcomed her with a hug. She had the face of an angel; a long face, with yellow curls framing her face and blue eyes resting on my mother. Then she looked at father and me, bowed her head in salutation and told us how happy she was that we came to celebrate together, as a family, the end of the mortal life and the birth of the eternal one. She took us to a large amphitheater and asked mother to say goodbye to us and to prepare for a new rebirth in the forever lasting world of next."

Allan remembered his mother, who had turned to him and opened her arms to embrace him, her dark eyes sparkling with excitement for the first time that he could remember. He hugged her tight, tears running down his cheeks, and trembled in fear of losing her forever. Finally understanding what was going on, he asked her to please change her mind, but she looked deep in his eyes turned upwards to hers and whispered, "Soon, my son, soon we'll be reunited. This world is but a second in eternity." She let go of him to say goodbye to Father.

Father held her in his arms and breathed her in, but said nothing. His eyes were dead. Allan knew what he was thinking because he was thinking the same thing. She did not love him enough. She did not love either of them enough to keep on living.

He put his arm around Allan's shoulders and they stood together, drowning in mutual feelings of inadequacy and loss.

"Mother took a seat at the front of the amphitheater. We were her only audience, for she did not want others to accompany her on her final journey. She looked at the huge screen in front of her, which was showing an immaculate park in front of a majestic building with tall, marble columns. We stood at the back and waited for the procedure to start. Father grabbed my hand and began to squeeze it a little too hard, but I didn't want him to let go."

Allan remembered several people in white robes coming in with instruments on a cart and started to work around her, hooking her up to all kinds of receptacles protruding from around her armchair. They spoke in low voices to her, asking several questions regarding her last wishes and the way she envisioned herself in her future plane of existence.

"I only heard fragments of the conversation, but I could see her beautiful profile, her long dark hair framing her graceful face and the beginning of a smile, the corner of her lip raised in pleasant expectation. I wondered how someone could be so sure of life after death. I could not think of any reasonable answer. I looked up at father to ask him, but the question died on my lips once I saw the strain on his face."

With an involuntary shudder he recalled the memory, the image on the screen coming to life, and he could see several people in white robes coming out of the building and walking towards them. Mother moved in her chair as if she was trying to get up and move towards them, but the instruments around her immobilized her.

Then a robed person appeared close up on the screen, back facing them, and they could see the slim figure wearing that robe moving away and towards the people who had come to receive her. The figure had long, wavy, dark hair and she moved with a grace that seemed familiar to him. When she approached the others, she opened her arms and they all closed together in a tight group hug, as if lost friends had been reunited after a long absence. When she turned her face towards the camera, he could see the face of his mother, the way she looked when she was young. "My god," his father gasped, "That's Lucia, your mother, Allan. Exactly like she looked when we fell in love." He dropped into a nearby chair.

"Indeed, she was my mother, no one else. She waived her hand at us, blew a kiss and then walked away with the others. The screen went blank and a voice announced that the ceremony was over."

The people with the instruments, who had been silent witnesses the whole time, returned to his mother, checked her pulse and declared her departed. They did not use the word dead, just departed.

His father went to her, placed a kiss on her head and a hand on her neck to check for himself that she had no pulse, then came to him. Allan was not able to go closer, not even to go touch her again. He felt numb and paralyzed, not able to move an inch. His father helped him get up from the chair he had sat down in when he moved away, and they made their way back home as if in a trance.

"We never spoke about her from that day on." Allan looked utterly exhausted, having relived every second of that agonizing experience.

"Oh, Allan, I'm so sorry." Jules almost choked on her words, tears flowing from her eyes. "You must miss her so much."

"This might sound cold, but not really. She made a choice and I still haven't forgiven her for it. It's one thing to lose someone in an accident or because of some incurable disease, but as it happened, she chose to leave. I miss the family life we could have had, but it hurts that she didn't even seem to want it."

Allan looked at Jules, feeling her so very close to his heart, and a deep need to hold her in his arms and forget about the past made his soul ache. Yet he didn't make any attempt to get closer to her and hold her. He could not forget Jules kissing Lan in front of the house on the day of the attack, followed by Lan's death. He had seen them well enough through the window, and there was nothing he could do; he couldn't compete for the love of this girl with a ghost, not when it came to Lan.

28

Tom was staring out the large windows of his study, his back to Serge. The beautiful landscape of his property oftentimes relaxed him, but his mind never stopped thinking of the complicated issues they were facing, each of them requiring his attention.

His thoughts had been focusing on a disturbing revelation brought about when he had ordered an autopsy of Thomas' body.

Jackie, the young coroner, had revealed that Thomas had computer chips embedded deep in his brain. She had said according to her findings, Thomas must have had these implanted when he was still in stasis. He had to have been very young, a fetus even, to be able to successfully combine the organic with the synthetic so seamlessly.

"Do you think he was in control of his mind or was someone else controlling his thoughts and reactions?" Tom had asked her.

"I don't really know," she had replied. "But given the intricacies of the electronic circuits in his brain, I can tell you that he was meant to be able to act on his own, yet still kept under control. He might have been connected wirelessly, it's hard to say. In any case, this is technology beyond my understanding."

"Do you know anybody to consult?"

"Dr. Jones is our most prominent surgeon here and the OR department head. He might be able at least to give you better answers, though I'd use caution since he could even be privy to such experiments."

Going over that conversation in his mind again and again, Tom thought of the course of action he would take, and decided he would start by talking to Dr. Jones, who he had known since he was a boy. When he had to decide whether to acquire his own clone, he'd consulted with Jones, then had ultimately refused. And yet, his copy had been developed regardless, and by someone who had wanted to do away with him, for reasons he still hadn't uncovered.

"Things are in motion, Tom," Serge announced his presence with his baritone voice. Tom turned around and greeted his comrade and lifelong friend with a nod.

"We are monitoring the movements of the most important members of the community, city council members included," Serge started. "Somebody must be aware of manipulated clones in our midst, but we don't have the equipment to detect the electronic components that identify them as such, not with so many distinguished people having all kinds of implants."

"We have to somehow single out the ones who have had their brains altered," Tom replied. "I saw Thomas' brain on the dissection table: his brain was clearly different from anything I've seen. The implants were done in the developmental stages as a clone, everything so deeply intertwined that it could not have been done recently. How do we detect that short of a CAT scan?"

"I don't know, but somebody has to know more. I don't understand why you're keeping this a secret from the kids. Why don't we ask Daniel and David? Between the two of them, they might have the answer."

"Maybe I'm wrong to do so, but I cannot bear to lose Allan like I did Lan." He turned to face Serge. "If any of them had any knowledge of such a thing they would have said something. Neither Daniel nor Jules were privy to such experiments. David hasn't mentioned anything. I'm afraid if Allan finds out, he'll be by my side at all times, trying to protect me. The farther he is from me the better. This is something we have to do on our own."

Serge shook his head. "Coincidentally, I also came here to tell you that I talked to Allan and he thinks we should try again, with the ideas you had, to hopefully penetrate the fog. It's time to find out about what happened to the world. If it's distance from him you want, this is a good option."

Tom nodded. "Agreed, but there are so many things to deal with. Our city needs so much help, without even knowing it. I don't want to spread ourselves too thin by trying too many things at once. What if we succeed in going outside and thus make the city vulnerable? For all we know, we're letting the forces that keep us in know that we have become aware of them. Maybe we should find out first who our enemy is from within, and then fight the enemy outside."

"What enemy outside? What makes you think there is an enemy out there? At least send out scouts to tell us what we're going to have to deal with. We cannot play this game blindfolded; we need the knowledge that gives us power." Serge fell into silence, as if weighing whether to continue or not, then he seemed to have made up his mind.

"Tom, brother, what's going on with you? We need your leadership and you seem afraid of taking any definite action. You are beating around the bush, going in large circles around the issues. What's troubling you?" The concern in his voice got Tom to start opening up to his old comrade.

"Everybody is expecting me to take charge and lead them to victory. But I'm not prepared for this. Who is? I failed the whole city years ago by not seeing through this web of deception, and I was in charge of city security. Then I spent months in hiding and planning my next move. I thought I was being decisive and yet, I got Lan killed. I'm starting to suspect my wife may not have been in control of her mind either, and I couldn't save her all those years back. What if I make mistakes again? What if I lose all of you? How can I live with myself after that? Go to Happy Endings? Our training was lacking a lot; we were all complacent and lived under a veil of a false security. I personally consider myself not up to the challenge," he ended in a weak voice, facing Serge, feeling his face sagging and his eyes stinging with tears.

"You are the best we have, Tom. The best of the best or the best of the worst, I don't really care. We all look up to you and we trust you. There is no one better, not even me," he winked, trying to lighten up the atmosphere. "Do you think that heroes are made of special material? That they have a magical essence or charisma or what have you, to surround them with a certain aura and to make them incapable of making mistakes? Guess what, if you read of such invincible and flawless people, you did it in fiction books or in records ordered by the victors, trying to hide their weaknesses.

"We don't expect you to do it all by yourself. How about you start by building up the people you trust, empowering them to be the best they can be? How about using all their minds and hearts to help our society, so we can grow inside from the little seeds of hope for a better future? Not all is bad in the world. Just look at what happens in the Scrappie compound. Those people are changed, they have a purpose now and they need all we can give them. Help them be more sustainable, don't just feed them; listen to Daniel and help them feed themselves."

"All right. There is no way out for me, not when you talk like that. Thank you, brother, I don't know what has gotten into me." Tom smiled, the heaviness from his voice lifted a bit.

Serge stretched his legs on the couch facing the desk, feeling a sense of relief. Tom took a seat at his desk and continued.

"Daniel and I talked about having some of the Servers who live in the Elites' compound go out to the Scrappies and teach them how to work the land, plant some vegetable gardens. It's still early in the season. Then we can ask the Elites to give away some of their fresh vegetables and even donate some of their animals, so we can have fresh milk and eggs and meat for the increased population." Tom felt excited with the beginning of a new plan, a good plan for a start.

"That's a great idea," Serge said. "It will get their lazy Server butts away from the Digiscreens for a change, and perhaps bring some new hope to them, too."

"But how are we going to alter their perception that the Scrappies are outlaws and freaks?"

"Start with short reports of little kids needing help and broadcast some video clips of a couple of gardens, such as the one attended by Mel, Jules, and Daniel. Show kids playing with little animals and people working together and laughing, then some dancing and group games, anything to attract them to go there and be part of something different."

"Not bad, for a military man," Tom felt his lips rise in a smile. "I have to talk to the guys, especially David, to see what his friends at the broadcast station can do, and with Daniel and Mel to see how we can manage the whole affair. Also, the city council will have to be convinced it's the right thing to do and that it will not jeopardize their interests or way of life. With their Servers and their produce being shared with the others, I'm sure that's not going to be an easy task."

29

Daniel watched Mel sitting in the shade of a large maple tree and marveled at the change in her the last couple of months. She was surrounded by people of various ages, from kindergarten age up to their early twenties. *She is so lively and kind and affectionate towards these people!* His thoughts were full of her as she began talking to the new students.

"Every plant starts as a little seed. For example, the one in my hand is a zucchini seed. We plant it in the soil by digging a hole, just like this." She made a small hole with a stick. "We put this seed in the ground and water it." She stopped a kid wandering around by the arm, so that he would not trample on the fresh spot in the dirt. "We also make sure we don't step on it."

"After a while, we will see a plant pushing its head up to the sun. In time, the plant will grow bigger and stronger, will make flowers, some little, some big, with all kinds of beautiful colors that will attract bees and other insects. The flowers will get pollinated, and thus the plant bears fruits that we can eat. The fruits have seeds inside them that will make more plants, and the cycle continues."

"What does polli... something mean?" a little kid, eyes open wide, asked.

"Pollination is the process by which plant pollen, a yellow powder in the flower, is transferred to the stigma," She held up a different flower, a field lily. "See this part here? This is the stigma. Pollen is transferred to the stigma by the wind or by insects."

"So they don't have a mom and a dad either," the small voice concluded.

"Well, we all have a mom and a dad, even the plants. The pollen is coming from the dad, and the stigma is the mom part. You came from a mom and dad, too, you just don't know them. And you know what, it's not really important anymore, because you have our own family now. Families stick together and nobody gets left behind. And you are loved, little munchkin." She grabbed the little kid and hugged him tightly. The others looked at the whole scene and started to smile, with the beginning of a new understanding dawning on them, a sense of belonging and of being treasured for who they were.

Later on, Mel and Daniel were sitting together in the shade of the tree in their backyard, everyone else having left for the day.

"Why haven't you gone home yet, Daniel?" asked Mel, her dark big eyes boring questioningly into his. "You have your life back, just the way you wanted it: with purpose, with morals."

"I like it here with you. I mean, with all of you," Daniel felt himself blushing at the unexpected implications of his words. He'd been thinking of her in particular, his long lashes almost touching the lower eye lids. "I feel more at home here than in the city. The simplicity of it all is really touching. Besides, the new people need me desperately. It may not be my specialty, but I took a lot of medical courses in college and I have a good understanding of their bodies and their needs. I like to study their behavior too. It's so comforting to know I was right all along, you know, about their humanity. But why haven't you gone back home to have a discussion with your parents? Maybe they've changed, maybe they've been looking everywhere for you."

"There's nothing there for me. They never loved me. I know it now, when I feel your warmth, your friendship; I have a new family: Jules, Allan, David, Tom, you."

"I'm sorry for what you went through. Come here." He felt his heart go out to her, and placed an arm around her shoulders, while she placed her head on his chest.

"The worst thing was that I had nowhere to go. I mean, there was no school to attend, no friends to make. Not real ones, anyway, just avatars in a virtual classroom. And nobody was allowed to reveal personal information as to where we lived, for fear somebody might come and break in and do us harm, knowing we were home alone. Why couldn't they have set up a real school for us, somewhere in the Servers' compound?"

"I think it was because the city leaders determined it was dangerous to have the Servers gather together and start talking about the unfairness of their condition, and even start riots, causing a social upheaval of our society. You know, the online courses started a long time ago, but they were for working people who appreciated keeping their day job while studying at night in the comfort of their home."

"It might have been true for them because they were living on their own, but not for us, so young and vulnerable. How can we make good citizens and learn how to socialize or care for each other when we never see one another?"

"That is a huge problem of our society. It alienates people and thus, we become very self-centered and addicted to the only social media we have at our disposal: the Digi and the broadcasts from all over the city, the reality shows, the games, the virtual reality and so on."

"And they forget to have their own dreams and to pursue them and they get depressed and impatient with anything that keeps them from escaping in the virtual world. I see your point, and I can see how harmful it can be."

"I wonder how come you never got addicted to the entertainment." Daniel felt his scientific curiosity aroused.

"We had only two large screens in the house. Mom and dad were always watching, and since they basically ignored me unless they needed me for various chores around the house, I started to read books, and I got a passion for the world they created in my mind, so I never really craved the shows. What about you?" she asked.

"My parents were very competitive and they did not allow David and me more than two hours of Digi or net watching per night, so we could finish our homework. After that, they gave us their own homework; they said it was to help us to excel in anything we pursued. Turned out to be a good thing, after all."

They sat there in silence for a while longer, seated under the tree, and Daniel felt at peace, as if he had finally found his home, with Mel so close to him, enjoying their newfound intimacy.

30

Daniel was sitting at his old desk, having finished looking over the latest lab report fresh from the analyzer for the third time. He had come back to his old office, not because he had missed it, but because he desperately needed to find out more about the food coming from the processing plant.

Could this be true? It's hard to believe someone would do that to the people. Maybe I'm wrong. But no, the results are clear. The proof is in here. What's happening to our world? He felt exhausted by so many days of intensive research and tests, leading the team of researchers and lab technicians Tom had put at his disposal.

Daniel had called Tom and David to join him as soon as possible because the latest test showed some very disturbing evidence. Unfortunately, it was worse than he could have imagined, while confirming the suspicions he had raised all along.

His thoughts moved to Mel and her transformation, like a chrysalis turned into a beautiful butterfly. *She's so smart, she should be a teacher. She's a natural. Can she possibly love me?* It had felt so good to hold her in his arms. He wondered if he was in love. He'd never felt like this before. But then, he'd never had time or patience for anything but learning. He thought about helping her get into college.

He tried to shake off his personal feelings and once again concentrated on the job at hand.

He heard a knock and turned to see his brother and Tom at the door and motioned them to take a seat, his eyes moving back to the report in front of him, as if the results had magically changed to reveal a better outcome.

"I can't tell you how happy I am to see you back in your lab," David confessed, lowering himself into the nearby chair. Tom took another chair and came to sit closer to his young friends.

"I have to say I'm happy too, but not for the reasons you might think," Daniel replied. "I feel I have a purpose in life, and I can make a good difference. I tried to remember old lessons from school and I had the chance to partner with some good friends from the old days to study the composition of our food. Thank you, Tom, for helping me bring them together. We found some interesting facts. As a starting point, do you know where our food is coming from?"

"From the food processing plant, where else?" David seemed perplexed by the question.

"Exactly. A fully automated facility that nobody has entered for as long as anyone can remember, as per my investigation. I asked myself how come even I didn't have the curiosity to find that out before. No matter now. The food comes pre-packaged, it's sold to the Servers and sometimes the Professionals, too. Right so far?"

"Yeah, they buy it online or at a market, so what's the big deal?"

"The big deal is that the food recipes of the autonomous factory have been altered. We found new chemical compounds in the food we tested that were never part of the original package. The latest tests we conducted show modified glutamic acid."

"What does that mean?" Tom asked with concern in his voice.

"The original glutamic acid has very little taste, yet when ingested, people think the food they're eating has more protein and tastes better. It does this by tricking their tongue using the umami taste."

"What's umami?" Tom seemed unaware of the term, which was surprising coming from a highly educated Elite man, Daniel thought.

"It's a little known fifth basic taste, totally different from sweet, sour, bitter or salty."

"What is wrong with that?" David intervened, obviously unfamiliar with the details of this particular item.

"People become addicted to food containing this substance," Daniel explained patiently, knowing that he had to try and be clearer for the benefit of his guests. "But the main point is that glutamic acid is a neurotransmitter that the brain uses to trigger various processes in the body. Thus, the cells get overexcited to the point of damage or death, causing brain damage to varying degrees, triggering or worsening depression, learning disabilities, headaches, fatigue, and disorientation."

"You said it's a mutated or modified compound?" asked Tom.

"Which could mean that the effects could be magnified many times over," Daniel replied. "We will conduct more research to test our hypothesis, but we have already seen manifestations of depression and complacency among our citizens. I'm afraid they might be linked to learning disabilities, which is something very commonplace among the Servers nowadays, according to a statistics report I ordered a week ago."

David took a moment to compose himself, with a look of consternation on his face. "What are you planning to do, then?"

"Well, we have to decide on the next step. I assume that means talking to the Elite who owns the food processing plant, and finding out who is behind this," Daniel proposed.

"I'll take care of that," Tom said, taking command of the situation. "This is indeed very disturbing news. On the positive side, now we are getting closer to solving the mystery surrounding the happenings in the city. I'll hold the owner of the processing plant personally accountable for everything that's been happening. Do you have any idea how long we've been exposed to that chemical?"

"I don't want to speculate," Daniel tried to be cautious, "but the downward trend is very gradual, which could mean that what's been happening here is not a recent development."

"Yet the city mice in your experiment showed dramatic and immediate degradation," David pointed out, somewhat confused.

"Let's not forget that their lifespan is what, one or two years? The effects took place over several weeks. Their metabolism is much faster, and perhaps they are simply more sensitive to the chemical. I'm sorry, I am speculating here again." Daniel stopped, realizing he was trying to defend his theory without backup.

"Agreed, let's not jump to conclusions," said Tom. "It's clear that we have a dangerous chemical in our food, which also happens to be addictive, therefore people consume more food than they should." Tom rubbed his chin in thought. "We may have to move up that plan we discussed about the Scrappies living more off the land. And yet we can't just remove our only food source from an entire class."

David moved in his chair, looking somewhat impatient. "Guys, I also want to share with you some very disturbing news." He stopped and took a long breath before continuing, as if a heavy load was on his chest.

"Do you remember when I mentioned the subliminal messaging inserted in ads? And the targeting of the subconscious mind to trigger a specific behavior to the advantage of the messenger?"

"I remember perfectly well," said Tom. "I said that knowing that this is a possibility will give us a strategic advantage. Has there been a development? Have you found something more specific?"

"Yes, I have. I'd like to show you some of the clips I have and the images revealed in them." David pulled out his tablet, turned it on, placed it on the desk, and tapped on one of the icons.

A commercial advertising an upcoming show appeared, featuring an attractive young woman. She was busty with long, wavy hair and wore a perfect white smile while explaining the rules of the new reality game.

At some point during the commercial, the bottom part of the image changed ever so slightly. They saw it only because David pointed to that in advance. The change was so fast it was easy to miss. It happened several times during the commercial.

"Now, look at the part with the changed hue. I'll show it to you frame by frame, and you'll be able to see the significance of it." David tapped in a few commands. A freeze frame appeared on the screen and showed an image so burned in Tom's mind, he had nightmares about it. It was the heavenly realm his wife, Lucia, had chosen over him and their son. The lush vegetation, the beautiful park with the great marble building, they were all there for him to see. Large words appeared at the bottom: *I have prepared a room for you in my heavenly house. Come, beloved!* Tom stood up suddenly as if his chair was on fire.

"What is this?" Tom exclaimed in horror. "It cannot be true!"

"But it is true. I saw the same image on the big screen at Happy Endings clinic, when I accompanied several of my relatives there, so I know what this represents: a call to end one's earthly life, with the promise of eternal heaven. I know what Daniel says, that after death there is nothing, but I personally am an agnostic. In reality, no one knows for sure. But no matter what you believe, this is huge, Tom. *Happy Endings* isn't just an empty promise, it's mass murder. We have to stop it, and we have to do it now. How many more people will die thinking it's their decision?"

"You're right," Tom agreed. "We have to take action. Let me talk to Serge first. In the meantime, find other examples to prove that this is indeed a conspiracy and I will take it to the city council. This has to stop."

31

Tom met with Serge and discussed with his old friend everything that he found out from Daniel and David. The pieces of the puzzle were coming together at last. They decided that Tom would call a meeting with the city council and there he would reveal all their findings and order a formal investigation. The time for waiting was over. He had one more thing he needed to know before that. He had to find out who was behind Thomas.

With the tiny package containing one of the chips retrieved from his clone's brain, Tom was finally on his way to see Dr. Jones at his office. The medical surgeon's voice seemed pleasantly surprised on the phone, and he had welcomed Tom's proposal for a meeting.

Better be ready to confront him head on, Tom was thinking. *No point on beating around the bush.* He wondered how he could make him talk, if he even had something to hide. *I'll just be straight with him*, he finally decided.

The front desk nurse asked him to go to the doctor's office on the main floor, second corridor on the left, and the last door to the right. Tom proceeded as instructed and in no time he knocked on the door and heard a voice, asking him to enter.

Dr. Jones greeted him at the door and offered him a seat in a luxurious armchair, in which Tom immersed himself with a sigh of pleasure.

"How are you, old friend?" Dr. Jones asked, and Tom felt himself smiling, thinking back to all their years working together.

"All right, thanks for asking. And how about you?"

"Well, I'm fine now, once I got over the disaster at the cloning facility. Such a pity, all the destruction. All that work in vain now. We have to start all over again, I'm afraid."

"I was never a big fan of the work being done there. If we're starting over, perhaps we should focus our efforts in making life better for everyone, instead of just the Elites."

Jones frowned. "I've been conducting research on various cloning techniques at that facility for years, my whole life's work is gone. What really happened, Tom? Who destroyed the clinic?"

"You heard the announcement. There was an accident, an explosion caused by some pressure vessels, probably oxygen tanks."

"Accident, my ass. There was no accident. It was sabotage, you must know that. You can be honest with me. We've known each other since you still needed your mother to help blow your nose."

"Yes, we've known each other for a long time. And since you mentioned it, you can be honest with me too. Did you know that I had a clone?" Tom's eyes bored into the old man's eyes, unwavering.

"Of course I didn't, you never ordered one," the doctor replied, holding his stare.

"Yes, we both know that, and yet someone broke into my genetic material bank and stole one of my embryos. Did you know about that?"

"Is this a simple question or an investigation? Because I'm not comfortable with your tone, Tom. I'm old enough to be your father."

"Sorry, doc, I didn't mean to sound like I'm accusing you of anything. The fact remains that I went through a very rough time lately. For the last four months, the Thomas you've been working with was a clone that stole my life away from me."

The doctor seemed taken aback. "How did that happen? That's outrageous."

"I'll tell you later. It's dealt with and done now. The clone is dead. And I had an autopsy performed on it. It's why I'm here talking to you." Tom took a chip from his pants pocket. "We discovered *this* implanted in his brain. Do you know what this is? And what it's for?"

Dr. Jones got up from his chair and came close to Tom's armchair. He grabbed the chip in his hand, looked closely at it, and then he gave it back to Tom.

"I haven't seen anything quite like it. Do you have a lead?"

"No, that's why I came here first. I want to go to the medical device manufacturing plant, maybe they built the product."

"That's a good idea, Tom." The doctor stretched leisurely, then said, "I feel like having a scotch, you look like you need one more than I do. Care to have one?"

"Sure. Neat, please."

The doctor went to the bar obscured in one of the cupboards, and poured two generous glasses of scotch, one neat and the other on the rocks.

The old man is getting soft, needing ice in his drink nowadays, Tom thought, while receiving his glass with his open hand.

They both raised their glasses to each other's health and Tom downed the drink he loved, which was especially enjoyable coming from the doctor's coveted stash. There was always something special about that scotch. This time, though, there was something amiss with the taste and Tom wondered briefly what it was before Jones began talking again.

"Now, Tom, let me explain some things to you," the doctor said, taking a seat on the edge of his desk, facing Tom.

Tom signaled the doctor to go ahead.

"Do you remember my son, Arthur?" Tom remembered the doctor's son who had died more than ten years before in an accident. "He was the best man I've ever known," Jones continued. "Arthur had a dream, a big and generous dream. He wanted to escape the limitations of our city. He was always sort of claustrophobic and he felt the constraints of the city and the ever present mist more acutely than the rest of us. Since we couldn't expand the outer world, he thought of expanding the inner world, as it were. Oh, how smart he was, my Arthur. Nobody came even close to his genius."

Tom remembered a different Arthur, a schizophrenic man, always watching his shadow. Still, he acknowledged the fact that the man had been brilliant. A lot of the games and virtual reality shows had been designed by him, and even at present, all the software was based on the platforms Arthur had developed, based on modularity and scalability.

"Arthur had dreamed of a connectivity of all the minds in the city, a network that would enable the memories and thoughts and feelings to be shared by everybody, so that no knowledge would be lost, no life would vanish without a trace. It was his way of securing a means of everyone living forever.

"His dream was so grandiose... but the society we lived in had so many undesirable elements, such mediocre minds, and such lack of depth and breadth of thought. It was beyond the capacity of the computer databases to store all the information, and rather useless in some cases." Jones stood up to look out the window.

"Instead of trying to save everyone, his idea turned to saving the best minds. Eventually he determined, based on statistical methods, that the civilization he dreamed of establishing was unsustainable, given the number of people." He turned to face Tom.

"Euthanasia thus became an integral part of his plan, along with the creation of the network of minds, living for the most part inside the virtual reality of the computer. Can you imagine living in a world where you could go anywhere you'd like, not restricted by mist or walls or anything at all? It meant creating programs that would allow the people to travel to exotic places, copies of the original ones that perished together with the earth we had lost, plus completely new ones, even going to distant constellations and immersing yourself in the stellar dust, if only in your imagination. He invented a computer chip that could be implanted in the brain, thus connecting everyone forever. The problem was that the existing human being has a hard time adjusting to a new implant, foreign to their organic material of the brain." Tom was starting to feel drowsy, but Jones kept talking.

"He asked me to help and together we developed new clones that would have their chip implanted at very early stages, thus making the connection stronger and less prone to being rejected by the body. It took a lot of experimentation to perfect the method, and we were never quite successful in creating a true network that would allow human beings to function both in the real world and the virtual world.

"So we settled for the further development of virtual reality, trying to capture as many talented minds as we could. At the same time, I proposed the use of addictive chemicals that would lead to the decrease of our population in a humane way, and according to their wishes. Arthur helped by *motivating* the people further through the use of subliminal messages, placed strategically in commercials and entertainment programs. The things we could have accomplished if he was still alive… Our whole world would be connected together, with only the best of us alive, with clones that would give us the chance to transfer our essence from the central database to an organic form, to experience the joy of living, and then going back to the virtual reality realm."

Jones knelt in front of Tom, his face a mask of madness. "Our spirits would live forever, back and forth between the real world and the virtual world. But for ten years, it's been only me doing the good work, and we're not there yet. And now the west wing lab is gone. What a pity, indeed."

Tom was shocked and he felt sick to his stomach, yet at the same time he could not help but feel fascinated and awed at the extravagant, grotesque, unbelievable ideas he was hearing.

Then he realized that, for the last few minutes, as he had been listening, he couldn't move his body.

Tom found his voice, finally. "I guess you do know about the chip I just showed you."

"The implant? Of course. It's based on Arthur's design."

"So you knew about my clone."

"My dear fellow, *I* implanted it when the clone was just a fetus." The doctor seemed very proud of his accomplishment.

"You're a maniac," Tom muttered as he tried to get up from the armchair. But his body had turned into stone, with no feeling at all.

"What have you done to me?" his voice croaked.

"Not much, don't worry. Didn't want to have you jump on me, or get away. You needed to hear my story. You have no idea how I longed to share it with you," the doctor replied calmly. "I knew when you declined to order a clone that you'd never see things my way."

"What are you going to do to me?" Tom asked in a shaky whisper, as he was losing control over his voice.

"My dear Tom, you are going to meet Arthur again," the doctor smiled, and Tom could see a syringe in his hand, approaching his neck. He felt it puncture his skin and lost consciousness.

32

Allan was back at the mansion he called home. His father had called all of them to meet him there, to discuss the latest developments, including the discoveries about the subliminal messaging and the food poisoning. Together they would work on a plan, not unlike they had done while planning the attack on the cloning facility and the taking over of the city security forces.

Jules and Mel had come as well. It was their first visit to the house and Allan could see how amazed they were, looking at the extravagant interior of the mansion, so different from what they were used to. *Why didn't I have them here before? The work in the Scrappie compound took all our time, and we never had a moment just for ourselves.* That would change. They could all live here. But somehow, he knew in his heart that the girls would not accept that offer. *They'd rather be out there, helping the people they care so much about.*

David arrived with Daniel in tow, and they too seemed awed by the expensive furniture and the generous size of the rooms, bathed in light, looking immaculately clean and airy. Serge was the last one to show up, and he seemed a bit withdrawn, with a deep crease on his forehead.

"Something troubling you, Serge?" Allan asked him. The answer was negative, yet Allan couldn't shake his feeling that the older guy was troubled by something.

They made conversation, nothing of consequence, as if they were all waiting for Tom before getting deeper into the important things they were here to discuss.

~~~

When he regained his consciousness, Tom felt his whole body on fire. Sharp shots of pain seared through him and gripped his brain in a red hot crown of intense agony. His body, tied to the operating cube, was covered in sweat and shuddered in spasms whenever his nerves were triggered by the impulses transmitted through the myriad of connections and wiring surrounding his body.

He could see two other people in the room: Dr. Jones and his assistant, a young, petite nurse, both concentrated on their tasks at hand. *How did I get here? What are they doing to me?"* He could not make a sound, nor move at all.

Jones, what's going on? He tried to form the words but could not move his lips. The nurse glanced at him with a detached look and continued the testing of the circuits. "Doctor, he's awake."

Tom's head was immobilized but he could move his eyes. Dr. Jones came into view carrying a surgical knife in his gloved hand.

"Easy now, you're ready to become one of ours," the doctor said, lowering his face close to Tom's. "Sorry to wake you up for this. I need to finish placing your implant and your neural reactions are better analyzed in an alert state. Not much longer now. We just have to turn you around to reach the cervical area of your spine."

The calm tone of Dr. Jones's voice nauseated Tom. *How can he be so calm while doing this to me?*

The upper frame of the operating cube lifted itself and rotated around its longitudinal axis, until Tom found himself facing down.

The pain of the first cut, right at the base of his skull, was almost unbearable. They hadn't anesthetized him.

They're cutting me open! Tom had never felt more terrified in his entire life.

He continued to suffer as he heard of various surgical instruments being called by the doctor to the nurse, in that impossibly calm voice.

Tom was screaming in his head because his vocal cords would not respond to the terror inside. *Help, help me, someone, anyone, God, please help me.*

Eventually he stopped thinking about anything else, feeling like a poor, tortured animal. All his humanity was stripped away and the primordial instincts soon took over. After what felt like an eternity, he thankfully lost consciousness.

~~~

Tom never showed up at the house. Repeated calls to his mobile were unfruitful. Serge tried calling him at the office, at the council building, at all the places he could think Tom would be, all to no avail.

"It's been an hour since the appointed time," Allan finally acknowledged. "I can't think why father would be late. He's a military man, he's never late for anything."

"What if something terrible has happened to him?" Mel sounded scared.

"He had enemies; didn't he say somebody was tasked with killing him? Who was the guy who saved him, anyway?" Jules asked.

"It was me," Serge admitted. "I intercepted an email with the order through the secure channels. We've been trying to find out who was behind the plot with no success. The only place I didn't call is Dr. Jones' office, at the hospital. I'm afraid that Tom might have gone to the doctor." He paused, and then he shook his head, as if trying to make up his mind about something, and continued. "Look kids, I have to tell you something you won't like hearing. We were hiding something terrible from you, something that Tom felt was best kept a secret."

"What is it?" Allan said, almost frantic.

"After Thomas was killed, Tom asked for an autopsy to be performed. What we discovered was a series of computer chips that had been implanted in the brain, presumably while still in a fetus stage. I wanted to share that discovery with you, but Tom insisted we keep it a secret." Before anybody had a chance to ask, Serge raised his hand to ask them to keep quiet. Then he continued. "You have to understand Tom's point of view. He was afraid that Allan might try to stay too close to him and get killed in case another attempt was made on his life. Tom thought it unnecessary to add another dimension to the troubles we're still trying to solve. I'm not saying he was right, because I didn't agree with him, but he is still in charge here."

Serge paused for a second, while everyone just stared at him, waiting. "That fact did not mean Tom was going to let it go. He planned on finding out more from Dr. Jones about what was going on, in the hopes that the doctor was privy to such information. So he decided that he would go and talk to Jones. If he couldn't find out anything there, he planned in talking to the manufacturers in the city, while asking for David's help."

"I wish he'd done it, talked to me first, I mean. Why couldn't he trust me, after all we've been through together?" David's voice revealed how disappointed he was.

"I'm sorry, David, it was not about you. This was Tom's problem, over-analyzing and trying to keep all the loose ends together in his hand. I know him better than any of you and this is what he's been doing his whole life as the head of Secure-It. You can't imagine how much information he's had at any given point in time. He confided in people only if he needed their advice or input."

"Maybe he's going to change his approach from now on," Daniel intervened. "Obviously, it's not working very well for him or for us."

"Let's not judge him just now, please," Serge insisted. "He's a good man, and he has to think of everybody's welfare. Anyway, he must be at the hospital meeting with Jones."

"Wait a minute," Allan had made a sudden connection. "When I got replaced with Lan, there was this surgeon in the OR. It must have been Dr. Jones. Why didn't I think about this before? He must be in the middle of this nightmare. He must know what is going on. He was the one who made the memory transfer."

"Are you sure about that?" Serge seemed doubtful.

"No, I'm not sure. I remember only sniffing an expensive perfume, which was somewhat unusual in a hospital."

"What did he look like?" Serge asked.

"He had a calm voice. And he called me a dear boy." Allan's voice became unsteady, as he remembered the tragic events he had been subjected to.

"That sounds like Jones," Serge admitted. "I could just be overreacting. Maybe we should give him another half an hour."

"No!" Allan almost screamed, surprised at the urgency in his voice. "I have a bad feeling about this. The best thing is to go to the hospital now and confront Dr. Jones."

"Have you lost your mind?" Serge counteracted. "What will you say to him?"

"For goodness sake, let's just call the hospital and ask if Tom is still there. They must have him on the visitors list." Daniel's suggestion made sense, so Jules picked up the phone and called immediately.

The call to the hospital revealed that Tom had just left, and that the doctor was in the operating room, performing surgery.

"That doesn't make any sense," Allan commented. "Father's mobile would work then. Yet he's not answering it. We're going to the hospital. Now!" he walked towards the front door of the house, not even caring who was following him. The terror he felt in his heart that his father was going through something equally spine-chilling as he had been through was more than he could bear.

"Wait!" Serge exclaimed. "We need to have reinforcements. If we're fighting manipulated clones, we'll be no match for them. I'll contact my men to meet us at the hospital. Let's go!"

33

After an undetermined time, Tom woke up and noticed he was lying down on his back. It was hard to say where he was exactly, deprived of light and sound as he was. He tried to move slowly, to check whether he was under restraint or even capable of moving and discovered nothing held him down.

He sat up, moved his legs to one side of the bed, and then patted his arms, torso, and head to check for tubes or wires. When he found none, he stood up and stretched his body slowly, arching his back and bringing his arms together to the front, feeling like a leisurely tomcat, eight lives left.

Then the lights came on and Tom found himself in an incredibly large room. All sides, including the ceiling and floor, were a gleaming white. His body looked so weird; he could not take his eyes off it: his skin was a translucent, metallic grey. It was as if he was something else, not human, but a sculpture of a man, a moving statue.

I must be dreaming or else I'm dead. He started to move one foot in front of the other, watching in amazement how his feet were creating circular waves on the soft floor.

Suddenly, the figure of a man began to materialize in front of him, pixels of various colors appeared in the air and came together to form a long, white robe. Eventually, the robe filled with the body of a pale, bearded man with a halo around his head and deep blue eyes fixated on Tom, boring into his soul.

"Welcome to the kingdom, Tom. I am your god, I.M. Surprised? You have been chosen. Transformed into one of my angels, ready to obey my orders and take them to the material realm."

"Angel? Is this the afterlife?" Tom was utterly confused.

"Indeed. Except that you have the privilege of going back and forth between here and your previous world. I will be with you wherever you go, and I will speak through your mouth and hear through your ears. Thus, you and I will never be separated."

Tom did not think he liked the sound of that. *None of this makes any sense. What the heck is he talking about?* "Where am I exactly?" he asked.

"Of course. Allow me to show you around." Though he did not seem to be moving, Tom felt the air around him changing and all kinds of images rushed by, as if he was hovering over various kinds of landscapes, each one more amazing than the next. Some were atrocious, others divine. Beside him, I.M. assumed a seating position on a newly materialized throne of intricate design.

After a few minutes, he addressed Tom. "This is just an overview of the realm. I'll show you my Hell first, so you can see what will happen to you if you choose to disobey me. I will remain here, so you can have a better view. But remember that I'm also with you everywhere you go."

Tom suddenly felt immersed into the reality of the landscape, getting lower and lower, closer and closer. He was able to see at an arm's length a multitude of three dimensional images in motion, and felt nausea enveloping him, caused by the speedy descent of the images in front of him.

The movement stopped suddenly and he found himself alone on the edge of a cliff, looking down in the abyss from which an unbearable stench was rising. In slow motion, the abyss moved towards him and he started to descend lower and lower into it.

After a few minutes of slow motion in a greyish light, he saw the ground, a rough terrain, and nearby, a red water bubbling pool in which naked people were trying to stay afloat, screaming at the top of their lungs.

On the ground, he stepped towards the pool and could feel the heat enveloping him, together with the terrible stench. With horror he realized those people were boiling in blood. Before he managed to scream, the view was gone and he started to descend further.

Tom arrived at a dense forest of a dusky color with gnarled and tangled branches. He could see monstrous creatures with broad wings and clawed feet, yet bearing human faces, lamenting upon the thorny trees. He tried to move farther away from them, but instead the forest came towards him in a rush and Tom broke a dead branch while trying to regain his balance.

A gush of dark red blood came out of the tree, which started to cry in a human voice, asking for mercy. Tom realized that it was not the monsters who had made the noise before, but the trees themselves, being terrorized by the creatures. He could see in the trunks of the trees desperate human faces sculpted in the bark.

Then Tom was rushed to another plane, deeper in the abyss. He saw a desolately arid land, with people weeping miserably while running from tongues of fire, burning their flesh to the bone.

Next Tom found himself on a stony field the color of rusted iron, where demons with long and pointy forks were cruelly beating and stabbing naked people, driving them like a herd of animals this way and that.

Further on, in a moat, people were smothered in an unimaginable filth of feces, climbing on each other, trying in vain to escape.

Deeper still, people were trapped upside down in holes drilled in stones, and flames came out of the soles of their feet, while tormented cries of pain and despair could be heard.

But nothing was more horrifying than the terrible throng of serpents, among which naked people were running hopelessly, screaming in agony. Their hands were bound behind them with serpents, while other snakes were wrapped around and inside their bodies, consuming them.

The bottom of the great pit came as a surprise to Tom. In the twilight he saw what looked like a large tower, but it was in fact a giant, bound in enormous chains protruding from the rock. His body was covered in metal spikes that were going in and out of his flesh, causing him great pain and a lot of blood loss. The giant had his head down to the ground but he raised it as Tom approached. The face looked very familiar to Tom. It was his own face.

How can this be? Is it Thomas, maybe? None of this makes any sense. And all of a sudden, Tom understood. He had seen most of these before in the illustrations of Gustave Dore, the French artist, which had given him nightmares when he was a young reader. They were in Dante's Divine Comedy, one of his treasured classics, which described the great Italian's travels through Hell, Purgatory, and Heaven, but essentially it was an allegory of the soul's journey towards God.

How well he remembered the verses at the beginning of Dante's Hell:

"Before me there were no created things,
Only eterne, and I eternal last.
All hope abandon, ye who enter in!"

Tom remembered now how familiar some of the tormented faces were; people he used to know, who had passed away, gone to the Happy Endings clinic. It was not hard to put two and two together. *All hope is not lost, after all.*

~~~

Allan and Jules, together with Mel, David and Daniel arrived at the hospital with Serge and his men. Security guards were posted at every entrance and the group entered through the ER sliding doors, proceeding to the reception area. "We're here to see Dr. Jones," Serge said to the receptionist.

Beside her, a tall nurse with a shaved head was looking scared through the glass panel, her green eyes growing even wider at the sight of Jules.

"Dr. Jones is operating now. He will be available in two hours," the nurse managed to say.

"What operating room is he in?" Jules demanded.

"N-number three," the nurse stammered. *Jules must know this woman*, Allan concluded.

They proceeded in the direction of operating room number three, ignoring the nurse's yelling as she tried in vain to stop them from breaking the hospital's strict rules.

As they moved along the corridor, all the lights went out. That took Allan by surprise, but all of a sudden the hospital's generators, hard-wired to the building, came to life, and the lights came on again.

~~~

In the depth of Hell's pit, Tom had suddenly realized that he was dealing with the results of the experiment he had been subjected to. The reminder of the excruciating pain almost made him sick. *So you want to play with me, master of the game?* Tom fought the urge to laugh out loud. This "deity" could not even create his own hell, but had to steal from a human? He knew this was an old fashioned case of intimidation. It had fed on all those minds of the Happy Endings people like a vampire and placed them in this mock Hell. *I will be the end of you.*

Tom remembered his father's words. "Tom, we must not allow machine to rule over man. This is what your grandfather always said. I have a way to control the artificial intelligence machines and you must find a way as well." He'd held up a small translucent box for Tom to look at. "Inside this box there is a device you'll have implanted in your brain so that, among other orders, you can give a mental command to turn off the power to the central computer controlling the city. In the greatest time of need, you have the power to control the outcome. This is your responsibility as the future head of Secure-IT."

Tom had carried the implant ever since, without anyone else even suspecting it. Now that time had come. Tom realized then that he was not unconscious, he was simply hooked into a virtual reality environment.

"Hey, I.M., where are you?" he called, in a booming voice.

Tom could see the colorful pixels materializing once more, clustering together to form the grandiose three-dimensional personification of the tormentor, this time even more gargantuan than the chained giant.

"What do you want, human?" I.M. asked, with disdain in his voice.

"Is this the best a god can do, steal a human's ideas and creation?" Tom asked, raising his head to be able to see the face of his nemesis.

"How dare you...." I.M.'s enraged voice almost deafened him.

"Oh, shut the hell up, you second rate virus!"

And with all the determination he could muster, Tom issued the mental command: MIDNIGHT ALPHA. Then everything went black.

~~~

Allan was the first to enter the room. He saw his father lying on the operating cube, seemingly unconscious. A nurse had collapsed onto the floor. Dr. Jones was sitting in front of the monitoring board with his elbows on his knees and his head between his hands, looking down.

He went to his father, checked for a pulse and felt a faint one. "Wake him up," he ordered. The nurse who had been running after them called for another doctor and together they injected Tom with something.

"We have to wait for a few minutes," the doctor said.

Serge went to Dr. Jones, still sitting limply in his chair, and checked his pulse. There was none. The man had died in that awkward position.

A few minutes later, Tom opened his eyes and set them on Allan, who was sitting to his side.

"Father, are you okay?"

"I am now," Tom said in a hoarse voice. "Is the network down?"

"A minute ago all the lights went out," Allan informed his father.

"The networks are down too," David said, after checking the computer terminal and his own tablet.

"Cut the power to anything computerized. We have to start over." Tom's voice sounded exhausted.

Mel, Jules, Allan, and Daniel gathered around Tom. "Are you going to be okay?" Mel asked, teary eyed.

"I'm pretty banged up. But it's over now," his father seemed very satisfied, in spite of his extreme fatigue and the ordeal he must have endured.

34

It took Tom a few days to recover. He still did not have full control of his movements, the fried circuits having caused slight damage. Still, he was ecstatic he hadn't died like the altered clones in the city.

Because of the shutdown, Elysian Fields had lost over a thousand people: poor, tortured souls at the mercy of an insanely disturbed entity. All the members of the city council had been found dead, along with a large number of prominent scientists and software specialists.

Dr. Jones's wife came forward with a terrifying confession that confirmed everything Jones had told Tom. She told them how all of it started with their son, a bright computer science major, who also happened to be schizophrenic. Her husband wanted to help their son overcome his condition and get rid of the chemicals he had used to keep his brain functioning somewhat normally.

Together they'd dreamed of a new race, bringing together the organic and synthetic, connecting the human mind to the cybernetic intelligence. They developed the prototype implant and attached it to Arthur's brain, enabling him to have exponentially increased capacity for game development and virtual reality manipulation.

They dreamed of a wonderful future for a new race of people, all connected together forever, overcoming the barriers of the current human mind. They began using euthanasia to control the population and take control of the fate of the city.

Ten years ago, their son had died in a freak accident, a power overload as he was hooked to the network, and somehow things took a life of their own. Dr. Jones managed to connect to the central processing unit, as he had seen it done by his son, and became aware that an artificial intelligence entity was trying to connect with him.

Whether it was related to his lost son or was not, he never found out. But he had found an ally nevertheless, someone who could understand him and his audacious dreams. Together, they continued the manipulated clone development and everything else his newly found friend at the heart of the processor initiated.

Mrs. Jones had not been willing to play an active role, nor had she been ready to go through the transformation process of becoming altered herself. But she had never condemned him either, because she had loved him and she had kept listening to her husband's revelations with the slight hope that her son was not gone forever.

When the confession was over, Tom looked at Allan, Jules, Mel, David, Daniel, and Serge, all of them silent, stunned by the revelation.

Tom reflected on how atrocities are so often done in the name of a good cause, on the intricate capacity of the human soul for good and evil. The sincere desire of a father to help his son had turned on its head to control the fate of an entire population.

How can we be like this? How can we soar to the sky one minute and reach the lowest depths the next? The blessing and the curse of the human condition is in the choices we make.

35

Allan and Jules were waiting for Tom and Serge, seated against the back of the fence behind the Tom's large Elite mansion. As they waited, Allan started to tell Jules what he had found out from his father.

It was not by chance that the mansion was built in that exact location by Allan's grandfather. The back of the property had a southern orientation and was placed right on what used to be a major road leading to the former city. It used to be called a highway, Allan said.

Right after the quakes, Allan's grandfather had some of his soldiers stationed there and at other locations close to former highways, to protect the city from potential attackers if they happened to come to the city. It had seemed likely that the most preferred choice would be to use existing roads to penetrate the mist.

Then he built his own home there, close to one of the major entry points to the former city, to be close to his soldiers.

It made sense to them now, why Tom's efforts to go through the fog were always following the same path, since the former highway still offered a pretty smooth walk, and now a ride for the three members of the expedition to the outside.

"I feel so excited, my heart feels like it's going to burst open," Jules said, with her hand over her left breast. "Aren't you excited?" she asked Allan.

"Of course I'm excited, but you have to keep your feelings and emotions in check. We need clear heads for the mission. Stop fidgeting," he scolded.

So much for keeping your emotions in check, Elite boy, she thought, but her thoughts were interrupted by the arrival of the others.

A truck arrived and Tom climbed out first, holding a cane in his hand. He leaned on it, and started walking towards them. *Same old stubborn Tom,* thought Jules, yet she was happy to see her protector and friend up and about after his ordeal.

Serge was right behind Tom, and he ordered the soldiers accompanying him to unload the equipment needed for the expedition.

When they got to the other side of the fence, facing the fog, the soldiers opened the boxes and extracted three platforms on wheels, each wheel actuated independently.

"Are you sure you don't want us to wait until you're back to full strength and go out there yourself?" Serge asked Tom.

"I thought I told you guys. I'd love to wait a couple more weeks and accompany you. Unfortunately, I owe a great debt to the people in the city after all they had to go through over the years. I have to stay put and take care of the affairs of Elysian Fields before my own. If something happens with me out there in the fog, who's going to take care of them?"

"Just checking, brother. I know how much you dreamed of this day. We might succeed, you know; that is, if we don't lose our minds first," Serge looked a bit doubtful, and trying to encourage himself at the same time.

"Thanks for letting me go, Father," Allan said. "I know how hard it is for you to do that. And I appreciate your confidence in me by letting me take risks."

"As much as I want to keep you out of harm's way forever, I know it in my heart that you're not a boy anymore. Without you, I would still be in hiding. Time to let go, as hard as it is to lose control."

The moment of their departure arrived. Tom went and hugged Allan, then Jules. Serge offered his hand and Tom shook it, then pulled his friend in a hug, patting his back.

At last, Tom signaled one of the soldiers to provide Jules, Allan, and Serge with headsets which contained brainwave modulators and asked that they all lay down on a platform and strap themselves in.

"Why are we sending three people instead of one, again?" Serge asked.

"I told you," Tom replied, "if one of you is in trouble, another one can help. More so, the third one can potentially save the others, with increasing chances of success."

"How is that going to help, if all three of us are in such a panic that we would be incapable of doing anything and we die?" Serge replied. "I'd better go by myself; these kids have no clue how hard it is deep inside the mist."

Obviously he's trying to protect us, Jules thought.

"Serge, they're not helpless. Besides, they are young and bursting with energy and will have it no other way. Meanwhile I'm getting a bit rusty and unable to resist their requests." He turned to the others. "Second thoughts, anybody?" Tom asked, when Serge gave up trying to change their minds. "Now is the time to speak up if you're not up to it. There is no shame. Serge, it's okay to say no, if the strain is too much for you to bear." Tom's lips curled in a smile.

"Knock it off, Tom!" was Serge's answer.

They were going into the fog for thirty minutes while tied to the robotic platforms remotely controlled by Tom. They'd be knocked out by the modulators and once they woke up, they would make a decision based on whether the fog was still causing them to panic. Thus they could either continue ahead, driving or pulling the platforms themselves or, if overwhelmed by panic, they could signal to Tom to drive them back remotely while still in the range, activating the modulators again.

"Tom, I just want to say thanks for saving my boy's life back then," Serge said at last, sounding a bit embarrassed for bringing it up so suddenly in front of the others, surely knowing what a modest man Tom was. Still, he probably wanted to make sure his gratitude known in case something happened out there.

"I should thank you for all those years of friendship. Just get on the platform, all right?" Tom changed the course of the discussion, obviously nervous over Allan and Jules accompanying his friend.

"Nighty night, then," said Tom, and he turned on their modulators. The three immediately fell asleep.

~~~

"Hello? Anybody there?" Jules asked in the milky air. She started to untie herself. She could barely see her hand in front of her.

"Right here," Allan answered in a muffled voice, as if she had cotton in her ears.

"Good thing we tied the platforms together," Serge said sleepily, sitting up on his platform. "Do you guys feel anything, ants in your pants or anything?"

They were all feeling unexpectedly good. After all the preparations and the scare Serge had inflicted on the young ones, nothing seemed out of the ordinary. They continued with their plan and took control of the platforms, remembering to communicate to Tom to let go of the remote.

After less than ten minutes, the fog began to dissipate and the most beautiful view of their life appeared. An expanse of tall grasses, waving in the gentle breeze gave way to a view of a lush, green forest in the distance. A clear, deep blue sky filled their hearts with pure joy.

"Life is going ooooon!" Jules cried from the top of her lungs. "We are not doomed. Oh, my god, it's beautiful!" She jumped up and wrapped her arms around Allan's neck, hugging him fiercely, while he held her and twirled her around. Somehow their mouths found each other and Jules felt Allan's lips pressed against her in a fierce kiss, deep and hungry, taking her breath away. *Oh, wow, where did that come from?*

Dizzy with happiness, and quite embarrassed, she looked Allan in the eyes for a second, then she pushed him away to get a hold of Serge too. She brought them all together in a very tight group hug as if her life depended on it.

After that explosion of heavenly joy, Jules looked at Allan. He seemed lost in space for a few seconds, looking at her as if he saw her in a completely new light, then he smiled his gorgeous smile and grabbed her hand. They both let their eyes take in all the beauty of the new world they had discovered.

Serge looked at them with a gentle smile, and Jules could hear his deep sighs of relief and relaxation, as if a tremendous load had been lifted from his chest.

It was Jules who noticed a group of deer at the edge of a small pond.

"Deer! Do you see? There are deer!" A curious look crossed her face. "What are they doing? Can you see? Something is happening. Let's go and check it out." She took off towards the herd of animals. Serge called out, warning her to first check her surroundings, but Jules ignored the warning, too excited to start exploring. Both men moved after her, their eyes ready to spot any sign of danger. *They can take care of me,* she thought.

Jules got to the pond just in time to see a fawn stuck in the mud. All the deer scattered as she approached. They had been trying to nudge him to get out but were unable to do so. Without any fear that she might be attacked by antlers or hooves, she stepped in the mud and started to pull the fawn out by his front legs.

"Are you serious? Is that safe?" Allan asked incredulously.

"You have a better idea, get in and show me," she replied. He walked gingerly into the water and ended up just as deep in the mud as Jules.

Serge just shook his head, took his belt from around his waist and placed it around the fawn's neck and started to pull. By pushing and pulling, yelling and encouraging each other and of course the fawn too, they managed to get it out, all muddy but happy beyond description.

"That was fun," Serge admitted. "And for a good cause, too." He smiled at the fawn, who had already rejoined his family and moved away.

"What are we going do now?" Jules asked, after they washed themselves as well as they could, their clothes still very muddy and sticking to their bodies. "I want to go further, see what else there is out there."

"We can't go like this, all wet, dirty, and without any provisions or plans," Serge's voice sounded firm. "The mission was to see if we can get past the fog. We owe Tom and our friends an answer. What if something happens to us? We go back now."

"But, Serge…" Jules started.

"No buts, young lady," he was unmovable. "Our mission is accomplished. We go home now and one day, very soon, we come back with more of us and then we can start exploring to your heart's content, all right?"

When not even Allan uttered a word of support for her cause, Jules knew that she had no choice but obey, knowing in her heart it was the right decision anyway.

"All right then. Good bye, beautiful world," she blew a kiss towards the distant forest. "We have to go now, but we'll be back soon."

And they went back to their platforms to start their journey back home, to an end, to a new beginning.